Coming Up
The Driveway

<<>>

Henderson Frank Ponder

World Class Books

First Edition Printed 2013

ISBN 978-1-304-44751-7

Printed in the United States of America

In Memory Of The Girl I Love

BUNTON

<<>>

Dedicated to

My brood:

Claudette and Jenette

Jeremy and Terry

Reiner, Bragan and Kilie

Luke, Kate, Taylor and Aria

Jerry, Coleman, Mary Ann, and Eric

CHAPTER ONE

It's amazing how memories flow back when you reach eighty five... and it seems sometimes that the oldest memories come first. One of my earliest memories was when my daddy got his first job near the end of the depression. His new job was at the Berryton Cotton Mill in northwest Georgia. And our new home was a three-room cabin that Daddy built about two miles up the Raccoon creek from the village of Berryton. The cabin was built on the John Berry property. Mr. Berry also owned the cotton mill, the company store, and the entire village which consisted of approximately 100 houses. I think that we were probably the last family of squatters in Georgia.

Immediately after we moved into our new cabin, my parents joined the Berryton Church of God, and from then on our family was at that church almost every time the doors opened. We were always at Sunday school, and Sunday morning preaching, and at the after service dinner-on-the ground which happened most Sundays when no one invited the preacher home to dinner. We also made it to church for Wednesday night prayer meeting, to choir practice, and to all the other many functions the church offered.

And even now I can remember in vivid detail things that that preacher said back then when I was only six years old. I remember the story about the big fish that swallowed that fellow, what's his name... you know, the one that got puked up on the creek bank? And I remember how the preacher said that people used to have to kill a calf, or a pig, and cook it on some kind of bar-be-cue pit called an altar. If they didn't, he said, they would go to Hell. As a matter of fact that preacher was always saying that somebody was going to Hell. He said that the only way to get to Heaven was right there in that church at that altar. He said that a lot of people were on the wrong road... like them Baptists over next to the company store, and the little bunch of Methodists down by the creek. "It's a pity," he said, "that they don't know the straight and narrow way."

The rest of that fall it seemed to me that time was so slow. Of course I had lots of time to do things... to watch the pretty birds and try to figure out how they could fly... to catch worms and wonder why they curled up and looked sort of embarrassed when you pick 'um up. And I had lots of fun with my little puppy, Fido.

It seemed that Christmas would never come. But it finally did, and guess what? Santa Clause brought me a shiny new red wagon. And boy! That thing sure would go... specially when I drove it down the hill towards the creek.

Momma didn't like for me to drive my wagon towards the creek, but she didn't worry much. She knew that I could already swim pretty good... specially when she would hold me up. And anyhow, the creek on the side where our house was had a big sandbar that came plum up to the creek bank, and Momma had already told me not to get out on the sandbar. I didn't, but sometimes I would sneak down to where the sandbar didn't come plum up to the creek bank and watch the little fish, and sometimes I would see a crawfish. One time I saw some of them little things Momma called tadpoles. They looked funny.

After Christmas I started to wish it would get to be time for me to start to school, and it did. It seemed like time was finally catching up with me. Momma bought me some new overalls and a fuzzy coat that looked like a sheep, or Billy goat, and some new shoes and stuff and took me down to the schoolhouse one morning and told Mrs. Smith to make me mind. I did! When the bell rang and we all went in the school, Mrs. Smith told me to sit in one of the two-seat desks at the front. Then she got a pretty little girl to sit with me... her name was Mary Jim. Boy, Mary Jim sure was pretty. I already knew that she was my sweetheart.

Turned out that Mary Jim was about to start to the Church of God... I think her Momma had been taking her to the Baptist church. I asked her if she was going to heaven, and she said she was. I asked her if the Baptist preacher knew about the man that got swallowed by that big fish, and she laughed. I was embarrassed. Maybe our preacher was just telling a big fish story, and I got to wondering about all that stuff. How could Jesus talk to him when he couldn't even see Jesus? And if he did, why didn't he ever say nothing to me? Maybe that preacher was just telling all them stories to please the church ladies so they would cook him some more chicken. He really liked chicken. Maybe that was why he said some things that made them laugh. Maybe there wasn't no God, and no Jesus. Maybe he just made it all up.

As time went on and I got bigger and could think better and figure things out, I really got worried about some of the things that preacher said. If some people had to go to Hell 'cause they went to the Baptist Church, or maybe to the little Methodist church down by the creek, then what if they didn't have no church? What if they didn't know they had to go to the Church of God and get down on their knees and pray and shout and dance and stuff?

I started to get real worried about the niggers too. Now I use that word with respect. That's what everybody called them back then. My best friend was one. I don't think that the words Afro-American had been thought up that far back. My friend's name was Ira. He was the one that drove the store truck. Ira would always bring Momma some groceries on Fridays. And best of all, when he came to our house, he would always bring me a big old polished red apple. I really liked Ira, and specially them big old polished red apples.

One day I asked Momma, "Why don't niggers go to church?" Momma looked sort of funny.

"They do, I think... some do".

"Where they go?"

"I don't know for sure," she replied. "I think they have a church up at Summerville. Guess they walk up the railroad."

I thought about that for a moment. Looks like they would just come to the Church of God. It was much closer than Summerville, and besides that church at Summerville might not have a preacher that knew how to get people to go to Heaven. I looked back over at Momma. "Do niggers go to Heaven Momma?"

Momma looked real funny. "Well, they say that they are real people. I guess they do. I guess some of them do."

Finally, on Sunday the preacher was back at our house after preaching. Guess he was real tired from all that preaching because he kept scrunching up on the couch and looking back towards the kitchen. Probably wanted to get some of Momma's fried chicken in his belly and stretch out for a little nap.

When we got to the table and the preacher got through saying the blessing, I looked over at him and asked,

"Do niggers go to Heaven?"

"Some people say so," he snapped. "Would you pass the fried chicken, brother Ponder?"

CHAPTER TWO

Finally, after what seemed like a hundred years, Christmas was about to come. Mrs. Smith said we did not have to come to school until after old Santa Clause visited. Well... that was something that I had been hoping would happen for a long time. When we were about ready to leave, Mrs. Smith said that I was a pretty big boy now, and when we come back to school I would be in the first grade. She said that when we get back I should change to the other side of the schoolroom and sit with that other pretty little girl, Bettye Earle. Well... I didn't much like the idea of not sitting with Mary Jim, but Bettye Earle was pretty too, and maybe she could be my sweetheart. Course, I better not tell her. She might not like that.

When I got home, Momma was busy fixing things up real pretty. "Got to get ready for Santa Clause," she said.

She had pretty paper ropes and little scrunched up things hanging over the door and across the big room by the fireplace, and some big things that looked like bells 'cept they weren't bells because they also were made out of paper... and she had some pretty candles sitting on the mantel piece.

I looked out the door and screamed, "Look Momma! It's snowing!"

And it was. Great big things that Momma called flakes was falling all over the ground. "Boy," I thought, "This is just good. Old Santa Clause will like this stuff. He can make his reindeer and big old sled slide on the housetop real good."

But then it seemed like Christmas would never come. Daddy was busy making little tables and chairs and kitchen cabinets out of them wood boxes he brought home from the mill. Momma said he was making them to sell to some of the mommies and daddies down at town so he could buy some more pretty stuff down at the store. And Momma stayed busy most all the time fixing things up pretty and cooking some pies and cakes and stuff. On Saturday she said that she had to make some extra pies 'cause the preacher was coming to dinner again after church Sunday. "Guess he wants some more fried chicken and stuff," I thought.

Sunday finally came and that preacher came and ate almost more chicken and pie than he could hold, and Daddy said to Momma when he had gone home, "Ain't gonna have no chickens if that fellow comes a few more times."

And you should have heard what that preacher said at church that morning. He said that some children were running away from some bad people who was trying to hit them with sticks and rocks and cut them with knives. He said that the children ran hard and got to the creek before them other people got there... He called it a sea, or a red sea or something, but Momma said it was like a creek, and he said

10

when them children got to the creek that the water went back and them children ran across that creek lickety-split and that the water came back and that them bad people couldn't get across and they got drowned.

Now, don't that sound like a big bunch of malarkey? How did that water get to be red, 'thout them bad people got cut on them knives when they were about to drown? I decided that that preacher was just making stuff up so they would think that they had to go to the Church of God 'stead of over at the Baptist so they could get to Heaven.

Anyhow, it kept on snowing and when the night before Christmas finally got there, we all got in the big room by the fire and Momma got some cake, and pie, and oranges, and nuts, and one of them big old red polished apples that Ira brought, and we sat down by the fire and had a good time eating stuff. Daddy got a pot and put some popcorn in it and hung it over the fire and we all laughed and thought is sounded funny when it started to sizzle and pop. Boy, that popcorn sure tasted really good. Finally, Momma said we better get in bed 'cause Santa Clause would be flying over the big hill up behind the house any minute now.

I thought, "You reckon them reindeer can fly plum up there where Jesus is?"

But then I thought, "No, I don't think so. If they did, they wouldn't have no snow and couldn't get the sled to stop and slide on Jesus' roof... and what if they made a mistake and tried to land the sled on the moon? Wouldn't that make the reindeer's feet get hot?"

"Boy!" I thought. "There's so much stuff to think about... so many things to learn, and even if Mrs. Smith did say that I should ask questions when I wanted to know how things happen, I wasn't going to ask Momma and Daddy about that now, specially while they were getting us all ready to go to bed."

Finally, when we got in bed, Momma said to be quiet and go to sleep quick so Santa Clause could come, and I tried hard but couldn't go to sleep. Momma and Daddy stayed in the big room by the fireplace and fastened the door, and I could hear some banging and some stuff making a racket like Daddy might be hammering on something and trying to make some stuff get fixed better, and Momma would laugh and sort of whisper and Daddy would shoosh at her and whisper and I could hear what he said like, "Be quiet... woman! You'll wake up the dead."

Boy! I hoped that didn't happen.

CHAPTER THREE

It really was hard to go to sleep that night. I kept hearing Daddy make racket with that hammer, and sometimes Momma would whisper real loud, and Daddy would shoosh at her and she would laugh out loud. And about the time it almost got quiet, Jewell had to get up and use the slop jar. She almost stepped on me when she got down. I was sleeping on the little pallet thing Momma kept pushed up under the bed that the girls slept in.

"Better put that catalog back good," Rosa said.

Momma had told us to keep the slop jar covered real good with the catalog after Ben dropped the lid in the toilet. But lately that old catalog was getting mighty thin. Just had mostly them slick pages with pretty colored pictures on them. Boy! Them pages didn't feel too good when it was cold weather.

'Bout the time Jewell got back in bed, I thought I heard Santa Clause up on the roof. "Listen… listen," I whispered. But Rosa and Jewell didn't say nothing.

Then 'bout that time, Gertha started to cry and Momma had to come in and pat her on the belly and say, "Go to sleep baby. Go to sleep and Santa Clause will bring something pretty." And she did and Momma went back in the big room.

"Shoo!" Rosa whispered. "You cover that chamber pot?"

Jewell turned over to the wall and said out loud. "Course I did. Think I'm some kind of hillbilly?"

The chamber pot that Momma always called a slop jar sat in the corner of the bedroom behind a curtain Momma put across corner-ways. And it got to smelling pretty bad sometimes. 'Course Daddy and Ben didn't use it. They had to go out to the toilet even when it was dark. But with me and Jewell and Rosa helping Momma fill it up… sometimes it got real full.

Anyhow, I finally dozed off when them reindeer stopped tromping up on the roof, and I guess I started dreaming 'cause I thought I was sitting up on the moon and Jesus was telling me something. But then, I almost woke plum up and I thought. "Jesus don't talk to little boys… but I ain't little no more. But I don't think Jesus talks to nobody but preachers."

Finally, I opened my eyes and it was not dark in the room, and there wasn't any candle or lamp burning.

I looked over and the big room door was open and Daddy was down by the fireplace putting a big old log on it.

14

Then I remembered old Santa Clause and jumped up and ran into the big room and screamed. "Santa Clause... Santa Clause."

And sure enough, Santa Clause had come. There were pretty boxes with ribbons tied on them all around the Christmas tree Momma and Daddy had fixed in the corner next to the front door. And some more things that didn't have no box, but had some big old ribbons tied on them. Man! Look at that. One of them things that didn't have no box was a shiny new scooter. It was pretty red like my wagon, and the wheels looked shiny like the wheels on Mr. John's big old car. "Boy!" I shouted, as I ran over and tried to get it from under the tree.

About then Momma and the girls rushed into the big room, and Ben got up off of the couch and everybody was talking so much that I couldn't think straight. I got my scooter out from under the tree and Daddy came over and helped me fix the thing that made it stand up by itself, and showed me how to stand up on it and push with my other foot. Boy! This was good.

I got some more things that was in boxes. I got some new overalls, and a pretty red-spotted shirt, and another fuzzy coat. But this coat was bigger and more fuzzy. It looked like a real Billy goat, or maybe a heifer. When I tried to put it on, Momma had to come over and help me. Boy! It sure was big. Made my arms punch out like the limbs on that big old hickory nut tree out in the back yard.

"Look at Henderson! Look at Henderson!" Jewell said. "Looks like a big old Billy goat."

I didn't pay her no mind. I was busy looking at all my stuff, and rubbing my hand over the handle bar of my new scooter.

When the commotion was over and everybody got almost quiet, I noticed that everybody else got something. Jewell got a new dress and some shoes and a little shiny necklace, and Rosa got a real pretty red dress and shiny-like shoes that made her look like a movie star, I guess. 'Course I never did see no movie star, but I guess Rosa did. She was big now. She didn't even have to go to school... and, she had a boyfriend. His name was Budgy. Boy I bet Budgy was going to think Rosa was pretty. He wanted to take her to Summerville and see a moving picture, but Momma wouldn't let her go.

Ben got some stuff too. He got some short boots, and a fishing thing, and a BB gun. The baby got some fuzzy PJ's or something, and a rattler, and a doohickey that made a whizzing sound when you pushed on it. And guess what Momma got? She got a new chamber pot that had a good lid with rubber on the bottom side to make it fit the pot real good. And she got a dress, and shoes, and a bucket of real store-bought lard.

Daddy didn't get nothing. But he didn't care. "Daddy's don't need stuff like that," he said... sort of under his breath.

CHAPTER FOUR

It snowed hard that Christmas day and during the night. You couldn't hardly even see the creek from the front window. And I didn't get to ride much on my scooter all that week, and part of the next week while we were out of school. I certainly couldn't ride it down the creek hill and not even out in the chicken yard. I tried to get Momma to let me ride on the porch, but she wouldn't. She said I might fall off of the porch.

The best I could do was when Daddy pushed the couch and stuff over in the big room and let me go across the floor. But that didn't work out so good. One time I hit the wall and bent the front fender a little.

Boy, I thought. I wish we could just go back to school. And we did. But that turned out not so good too.

When we went back to school, there was still lots of snow piled up along the road. I wore my new fuzzy coat and pulled the collar up high around my neck and it was good and warm, but I couldn't hardly walk with that thing on. My arms stood out and I couldn't hardly get my hand in my pocket to get out my marbles. And when we got to school, some of the kids laughed.

"Hey, Hen!" Some smart mouth said. "You 'bout to freeze?"

I didn't say nothing. Sometimes it's best not to talk to smart mouths. Some people got to say something like that about anything.

Anyhow, when we went in the school, things got a little better... well, maybe a little. I remembered and went over to the other side and sat down at the two-seat desk with Bettye Earle. Only, when I did she looked like she didn't want me to. She scooted over and acted like she thought I was a gonna fight with her. Then when I looked over at Mary Jim, she looked out the window and wouldn't look back... I thought that maybe she didn't want me to get another sweetheart. Maybe she wanted to be my only sweetheart. I never did ask her about that.

But I guess the day wasn't over yet. When we went out on the school yard at recess, there was a new boy playing on the big kids' side of the yard. You could tell by watching him that he was one of them smart mouths. He stood to be a bully, like my daddy always said. He tried to punch all the other kids, specially the littler ones. I learned later that his name was, Hugh Don.

I got to learn more about Hugh Don when we went outside to eat dinner. Mrs. Smith called it lunch.

When I sat down on the steps and got out my box and got my biscuit and ham sandwich out to eat, Hugh Don and that other bully they called old Boss, started to laugh. "He's got a biscuit... He's got a biscuit," they chanted. "Poor boys can't get loaf bread. Poor boys eat biscuits... Poor boys can't get loaf bread."

Well, I didn't say nothing. Daddy said that you can't argue with smart mouth fellows. And, I don't guess you can...

Anyhow, when I started home that evening and was walking down Shady Lane, Hugh Don and old Boss ran up behind me and mussed up my hair.

"Look at the curly top, look at the curly top," they teased. But when I turned around they took off and ran back up the road.

That was a good thing too, 'cause I was about to fight them. But I don't think I would have. Daddy had always told me not to fight. He said that gentlemen don't fight. "So don't never start no fight." He said that I should never fight nobody. "But, if somebody tries to fight you, don't ever run."

Well, that was a pretty fluffy how-do-you do. If somebody wants to fight, and you can't fight with them, and you don't run... what you gonna do? Just stand there and let them bat you in the head? Didn't make much sense.

But that didn't make no difference. Almost every day after that, them two bullies would hassle me on my way from school. 'Course they didn't tease me no more about my biscuit. After that, I started to eat my biscuit sandwich on the

19

way to school. That didn't matter none anyhow, 'cause Daddy always gave me a dime each morning, and I could run across the field to the store and get me a Moon pie and a R. C. cola. That was pretty good stuff.

But I didn't have much fun rest of that school year. 'Course, I would play with my scooter, and my wagon, and with Fido when I got home, and that was more fun than eating biscuits and ham and running after some old ball at school. And it was sure more fun than wanting to fight, or to run, and couldn't.

One day when Uncle Otis came up to the house and me and him was walking down to the creek, I asked him about that. "If somebody wants to fight and you can't fight, and you don't want to run," I asked. "What you gonna do?"

"Why you ask that?"

"Cause Daddy said not to fight, but he said if somebody wants to fight, not to run. He said gentlemen don't fight."

"Well he's right," Uncle Otis said. "If two gentlemen tried to fight, they would put up their dukes and say, Come on... dare you to hit me." He spat out a wad of tobacco and continued. "Thing to do," he said, "is to hit the sucker first, but not with your fist. Thing to do is to pick up a stick or a rock and bust the sucker in the head."

"That don't seem right," I said. "What if I was to kill somebody? Preacher said you would go to Hell if you do that."

"You ain't gonna kill nobody boy. You just crack the sucker in the head, and he'll leave you alone."

Sure enough, it happened just like that. Well, maybe not exactly. One evening when I was walking down Shady Lane, and got almost to the bridge, old Hugh Don and Boss and another big bully boy jumped out from behind a big trash box and started to hassle me. Hugh Don mussed up my hair, and old Boss put up his dukes and hissed. "Want to fight, pretty boy?"

Well, about that time, I did. I grabbed old Boss by the ears and pulled him up close and spit my chewing gum in his face. Then, I got my arms about halfway around his neck... couldn't reach all the way around because of the big fuzzy coat, but I hugged him best I could and we fell down on the ground and started to roll down the side hill, you know, the one that goes down to the spring-house, and we just kept on rolling till we got almost to the bottom. Then, when we got stopped, I got off of him and first thing I saw was a stick. It was one of them big old oak broom sticks that they use on them brooms in the cotton mill.

Old Boss looked around for his buddies, and when he discovered that they were still at the top of the hill, he started to run. And if you had known old Boss then, you would have been surprised at how fast such a pudgy kid could climb up Springhouse hill.

CHAPTER FIVE

The rest of that school year went by kind of lickety-split, except for when Hugh Don, and old Boss, and sometimes that other smart mouth fellow tried to hassle me. 'Course old Boss didn't hassle me much, thout Hugh Don was with him. Anyhow I would hurry home after school and play with Fido, and ride my scooter down the hill, not the creek hill; you know... the one that goes down to the barn. And sometimes I would get my wagon and ride it down too. Me 'n Fido played like we were gonna catch a rabbit, sometimes.

Finally, my birthday got to come. Momma said I was a big boy now 'cause I was seven years old. And Mrs. Smith told everybody it was my birthday. She got some cake, you know like Momma said was cupcakes... that's funny, and she put some on the big table and some of them little paper things like aunt Cordy puts on her table and she got a little candle and put it on one of them, and she put it on the table in front of me. And then, she got a match and put it on that candle and made it burn, and said "O.K... everybody sing." And they did.

Well, finally school got out and it got warm and I didn't have to wear that big fuzzy coat anymore. Me 'n Fido got to go down to the creek and Momma said we could get on the sandbar and catch some crawfish. We did. I mean we saw some... but we didn't catch any of 'um.

But the funniest thing that happened that year was when Daddy started to preaching. Well, it wasn't all that funny, but it was a big surprise. I didn't know Daddy was a preacher. I knew that he could testify good sometimes when that other preacher would shut up and let him, but I didn't know Daddy was a preacher. 'Course I thought something was going on. Daddy had been going somewhere and wouldn't come home 'till almost dark sometimes. I guess he was learning how to preach. Boy! I hoped he wouldn't tell them big whoppers like that other preacher told.

Anyhow, when we found out about Daddy being a preacher was one day when Momma said that we had to get to church early. She said that it was a special church time and that we would all be surprised. And, we were.

That night when everybody stopped singing and clapping and shouting, and stuff... that other preacher got up and said, "We have a big surprise for everybody tonight. We have a brand new preacher. Brother Ponder," he continued, "has been ordained as a preacher." Ordained! That's a funny word.

And then he got Daddy up there and they shook hands and Daddy started to preaching, and everybody started to say amen and looked at each other and smiled and said amen some more and Daddy kept on preaching and somebody got to shouting and somebody else did and, boy... it was funny.

I had lots of fun that summer. One of my favorite things to do was when Mr. Pickle would come up the little road by our house in his mule wagon to work in his cornfield which was about a half mile further up the creek. Mr. Pickle called me the "stiff-legged man." That's funny!

Anyhow, Mr. Pickle would stop his mule wagon up at our house and sometimes Momma would get him some cake and him and Daddy would sit on the porch and talk 'n stuff, and then Mr. Pickle would say... "Come on stiff-legged man. Let's go plow that cornfield." And then he would put me up on his mule wagon and let me get one of them ropes and drive that old mule wagon. Boy! I bet Old Boss can't drive no mule wagon.

And one time when Mr. Pickle was plowing in his cornfield, a momma rabbit jumped up and skittered off 'n me and Mr. Pickle went over there where that rabbit jumped up and found two little baby rabbits. Boy! They were pretty. Fido tried to bite one of them and it skittered off like its Momma did, but Mr. Pickle got the other 'un and let me hold it and said that I could take it home and keep it. And I did.

Another thing that was funny that summer... well, not much funny, but some... was when Momma said that the preacher got the croup and Daddy got to preach again down at the church. And it happened just like I was afraid it would... I mean, Daddy told one of them big whoppers. He said that there was a big fat man that could fight anybody. He said that fat man was a real big giant that could beat up a whole bunch of people and slay them... whatever that means... and that he could knock their house down with his fist, something like that. Then he said that big fellow needed a haircut real bad, and when his momma cut it all off he couldn't fight no more.

Boy! You believe that stuff?

Anyhow, lots of other stuff happened that summer. And one of the good things was when Mr. John would come up to our house. Mr. John would always bring me a poke full of candy. Mr. John first started to come up to our house and ask Daddy if it was alright for him and his friends to camp out down at the spring and cook some bar-be-cue and stuff. And then on Friday evenings, some fellows would come up the creek and bring some tents 'n stuff and fix a fire pit 'n stuff, and then on Saturday Mr. John and some more men would come and they would start to cooking. Me 'n Jewell sometimes would sneak out and peep down and see what them men were doing, and one time they had some brown bottles and was drinking something out of them. Well, me 'n Jewell knew not to drink out of brown bottles. Momma told us that.

Then, after a while Mr. John got to coming up to our house by himself and him and Daddy would sit out on the porch and eat some of Momma's black walnut cake, and talk. Sometimes they would get a pole and go down to the creek, and one time Mr. john caught one of them big old sucker-fish's... and boy did he jump up and down.

Well, I didn't think there was anything strange about Mr. John and my daddy being good buddies. Him and Daddy were plumb growed up like Momma said, and could be buddies if they wanted to. They were 'bout the same size and sort'a looked alike, some… 'Course Mr. John was older than Daddy, and he didn't wear britches like Daddy did… matter of fact, Mr. John's britches made him look sort'a like that preacher. But they both had big old cars that could skitter up that old wagon road at our house lickety-split. But Mr. John's car looked some different than Daddy's did. It had all four fenders and shiny wheels like my wagon. Daddy's didn't.

Actually, it was several years before I realized just how strange it was for these two men to enjoy each other's company. You see, Mr. John was perhaps one of the wealthiest men in Georgia. Daddy wasn't.

CHAPTER SIX

The next school year got there and almost went before any stuff happened. 'Course I was big now and was in the second grade and got to sit in my own desk. We had a new teacher that year... her name was Miss Woods. Miss Woods was actually Mr. John's niece. She lived at the top of Bradford hill with Mrs. Bretherton who was Mr. John's sister-in law. Phew... that's a big 'un.

Miss Woods sure was pretty. And, I think she wanted to be my sweetheart, but I already had two sweethearts. I figured that was enough. Fellow don't want to over do stuff like that, you know.

Anyhow, like I said, things went pretty good that year. Hugh Don and old Boss got busy harassing some more little guys like Jack Pool, and that 'n they called "Faye." 'Course, Faye wasn't really no Guy. She was a girl, and one could say that she was a real sassy girl. One time she picked up a rock and hit old Boss in the head. Boy! That was funny.

When my birthday got there, Momma said that I was getting just about too big for my britches. I was eight years old. She started to bake a big old cake, and when Daddy got home, he looked over at me and said, "Guess me 'n you ought to sally down to the store." And we did. When we got down there, Daddy told me to sit down on the hitching rail... you know the place where people used to hitch their mules, but they hardly didn't no more 'cause Mr. Cleghorn didn't like mules... sometimes they mess up stuff. Well, I got up on that old hitching rail and waited, and it wasn't long till Daddy came back out of the store with me a big old ice cream. Bout that time them niggers came up... you know, them that lived up at the graveyard, and the momma nigger got up on the store steps at the back door and that other one... you know the little one, he sat down on the bottom step. And when he saw me licking on my ice cream, he sort 'a started to licking on his chin. I held out my ice cream and said, "Want 't lick mine?" and he got off the step and came over and was about to get a lick. Then, his momma said, "Charlie! You get over here boy. Don't you be licking that white boy's ice cream." And he did... he went back where his momma was and sat back down. Finally, after a while Ira came out of the back door, and he had a ice cream and gave it to Charlie's momma... and then, Charlie and her started to lick it.

Boy! Old Ira was good. Boy, I sure hoped he would get to go to Heaven... and, I hoped that Charlie and his momma did too.

Anyhow, when me 'n Daddy got back home Momma had that big old cake cooked, and we all got around the table and everybody... everybody but me, started to sing that happy birthday song and Daddy went out to the corn house and got a big old box, and when it got open, guess what? It was a brand new Sears Roebuck guitar.   Boy! That was good. Momma said that Daddy paid four dollars and ninety-five cents for it. Boy! That's a lot of money.

Well, I got to picking that thing and couldn't hardly stop.   And then, come Sunday after church, my big cousin 'Boyce' came up to the house and he showed me how to pick a D... that's a chord.   And then he showed me how to pick a C, and a G, and said he would come back later and show me some more. Boy! Picking sure was lots 'a fun.

Finally, when school was out that year, Daddy made me some rabbit boxes, and me 'n Fido would take them up in the woods and put some corn and cabbage in them and fix that little hickey that made it catch a rabbit. Boy! We had lots of fun doing that.   One time I caught a 'possum and then one time I caught a coon. Boy! That thing like to bit my finger.

Another thing Daddy let me do that year was to take some boxes of candy and go down on Shady Lane and sell it. Daddy had lots of ways to make money. Momma said that some people down in the mill town thought we were poor. But we weren't. Matter of fact, Daddy always seemed to have lots of money. He had a candy business up in the cotton mill. Up in the mill Daddy had a sort 'a cabinet where he kept boxes of candy. It was many years later that I learned how that venture worked. Daddy would keep the cabinet stocked with candy and place a tablet and pencil in it for customers to record their purchases.   Imagine doing business that way today.

Another way Daddy made money was selling cars for the Ford place in Summerville. Mr. Alred would let Daddy drive a nice car home and keep it until he sold it. And then he would get another car.

In addition to that, Daddy would buy young calves and pigs and get them good and fat and butcher them. Then he would carry the meat down town and peddle it out. Sometimes he would order Sea Food from a Seafood market in Rome. Then, late in the afternoon when the train returned to Berryton on its daily round trip from Chattanooga to Rome, we would all go down to the depot and the man at the depot would put Daddy's stuff up on the platform and before long, all the fish, and shrimp and oysters were sold. And of Course Daddy still had his wooden toys workshop.

CHAPTER SEVEN

By the time I was fourteen years old, I was picking that old Silvertone guitar pretty good, if I do say so myself. Daddy was still preaching some at the Church of God in Berryton, and sometimes we would go to other churches where Daddy would preach... and, me 'n him and Momma would sing. Sometime later, when my little sister Gertha was old enough to chime in, she would sing too. People started to tell us that we sounded just like the "Chuck Wagon Gang"... a country-western group that was popular on the radio at that time.

But that's getting the cart before the horse, as Momma always said.

About that time, Daddy ordered me another guitar, a beautiful curved-top job this time, another Silvertone... and my dreams turned more and more to the day I would become a famous radio cowboy like Gene Autry and Roy Rogers.

But radio cowboy or not, for the time being it seemed, I was still a little short of being a full-grown man with the right and capacity to make my own plans. I still had to cope with the ordeal of going to school, and worst of all I still had to deal with old Hugh Don and Boss.

But then, one evening as I sat quietly at my favorite brim hole fishing, the problem of Hugh Don and Boss was solved. Just as I saw my cork bob up and down and reached for my pole, I saw old Boss and that other smart mouth fellow Chatman coming up the creek bank, and I knew that Hugh Don would not be far behind.

Old Boss and Chatman stopped just before they got to where I sat and started to play their usual game of mumblety-peg. I stood up and propped against the piece of two by four which I had nailed to the old cottonwood tree earlier. Then I glanced around and spotted Hugh Don creeping through the line of brush that grew between the plowed field and the creek bank. I guessed that they were about to repeat the thing they had done last week when Hugh Don came up behind me, grabbed and held me while the other two punks emptied my bait-bucket into the creek and cut my stringer.

But this time when Hugh Don came up behind me, I was prepared. I knew that Hugh Don was there, but Hugh Don didn't know that that old piece of two by four I was leaning against was about to come loose from that old cottonwood tree.

The next morning at Sunday school, I heard that Hugh Don had fallen from old man Kahilie's barn loft and hurt his head. Chatman and Boss had been there to witness the accident.

Another important thing that happened that year was shortly after Daddy got that big old jukebox-like radio. One evening we all sat in the big room and listened as Gabriel Heatter announced to the world that the Japanese had all but destroyed the entire U. S. fleet of warships at Pearl Harbor. Boy! That sure changed my plans to become a big-shot radio cowboy.

In any event, soon thereafter we moved to Douglas Georgia where Daddy was called to pastor a small church. Well... actually we stayed in Douglas just long enough for me to fall in love. My new sweetheart was a pretty little blond headed gal like Mary Jim. Her name was Mary Frances. And, although she was only fifteen years old, her daddy who was a somewhat wealthy tobacco farmer allowed her to drive his big-old 1939 Lincoln Zephyr. Boy, we had lots of fun. But then, and I never did ask Daddy why... but then, we moved back to Chattooga county and Daddy started to build a new house at 310 South Edmonson Street in Summerville.

At that time, it seemed that all the young men were going off to war. The radio was constantly booming with the resonant voices of Gabriel Heatter, Edward R. Murrow, and other commentators telling about the horrible atrocities being committed by the Japanese and the Germans. And I started to dream about the day I would sit on the back of one of those big old Sherman tanks and ride into Berlin firing one of those big old water-cooled fifty caliber machine guns.

However, my mother had other plans. She had long hoped that I would grow up to be a preacher. And, almost without consideration for my own dreams, she and Daddy had already started to plan for my education at BTS, a small church school which was destined to become the full-fledged liberal arts college and theological seminary, known as Lee College, at Cleveland, Tennessee.

CHAPTER EIGHT

The next year just after my fifteenth birthday, we moved into our new house in Summerville. At about the same time the new Church of God on Bellah Avenue in Summerville was completed, and Daddy and Momma moved their membership there.

By this time, I had started to read the Bible often, trying I guess to figure out the truth of all the Christian teaching I had absorbed over the years. And, I was still confused about some of the things I had heard in church and read in the book. For example, if the Ten Commandments were really true edicts from God, why did many who claimed to be men of God often break them?

For example: *"Thou shall not covet your neighbor's wife, or his manservant or maidservant, his ox or donkey, or anything that belongs to your neighbor."* Well, I didn't know so much about oxen and donkeys, but I knew for a fact that I had witnessed one preacher coming very close to coveting another man's wife.

However, the one that bothered me most of all was, *"Thou shall not murder."* Or in other readings, *"Thou shall not kill."* Boy! If that was the final word, there sure would be a lot of Japs and Krauts in Hell. And what about our own guys, they were starting to do the same thing. According to Gabriel Heatter, U. S. and British forces had recently wiped out a full battalion of Germans at El Alamein in Morocco.

This bothered me a lot. It was a sure thing that I was going to get myself into some branch of military service as soon as possible. All the young men, at least those who were eighteen years old were beginning to either volunteer or register for the draft. Budgie had already joined the Marine Corps, and many others known to our family were already in uniform, and there was no way that I was going to be left out.

However, knowing that I would soon be serving my country in a war that nobody seemed to understand, brought to mind the dreaded fact that a soldier's job is to kill the enemy. And in my mind, that still guaranteed one a ticket to the everlasting pit of fire. And even if, as an almost grown man of fifteen I was a little embarrassed to ask questions about such things, I still adhered to Mrs. Smith's edict. So consequently, I walked down to the church and asked the preacher.

"Preacher, what do you think about killing somebody?"

"The Bible says, *Thou shalt not kill,"* he replied.

I almost told him that I already knew what the book said about killing, but I checked myself and asked, "What about war, preacher? What about being in uniform and doing what soldiers are required to do? What if I go into service and find it necessary to kill someone." I paused, and the preacher turned towards the door and watched a car pass and picked his hat up from the piano.

"I guess," he said. "I guess, a fellow has to do what he has to do."

Well, that wasn't a very satisfying answer. I already knew that a fellow has to do what he has to do. But I decided not to breach the subject with Daddy. To do so would alert him to the fact that I was thinking about joining some branch of the armed services. And Daddy wouldn't like that.

In any event, there were many things going on to take my mind away from my plan to become a brave and celebrated hero. Mary Jim's family had also moved to the county seat, and we seemed to still have a certain rapport. We would often meet at the fountain at Jackson's drug store and share a banana-split, along with the company of other boys and girls our age. As a matter of fact, it was there that I met another blond that took my eye. And like the one in Douglas, her name was Mary Frances. Boy! Mary Frances, and Mary Jim and Mary Frances again. By then I had almost forgotten Bettye Earle.

It was amazing how much alike this Mary Frances and the one in Douglas looked. And, it was somewhat amazing how quick my interest turned from my old sweetheart and friend, Mary Jim, to the new blond in my life. Mary Frances had a job down at the Dixie Five and Dime, and she would ride into town in the mornings and go home on one of the new Victory buses. And it didn't take long for me to arrange to sit with her at Jackson's. Because I was concerned that Mary Jim cared... I arranged for my friend Leonard to be present to entertain Mary Jim when possible. And guess what? Leonard liked that.

CHAPTER NINE

Finally, my sixteenth birthday arrived. Daddy had already been letting me drive the Ford under his supervision. We would go down Possum Trot road and he would let me drive up and down between Berryton and the little community we called Possum Trot. And then, on the day after my birthday, I applied for my license.

Boy, this was great. I guess I was just about the only sixteen year old in Chattooga County whose daddy would trust to drive the family car. On Saturday evenings I would pick up Mary Jim, and Lou Cindy, and Leonard, and sometimes after work hours at the Dixie Five and Dime, Mary Frances, and we would drive around Summerville and usually stop at Willow Spring where the girls seemed to enjoy a little hugging, and sometimes... you know, kiss-kiss.

I knew that I would be going into service soon, and decided that a fellow needs a gal to wait back home for his return. Consequently, I convinced Mary Frances that we should become engaged... and without either of us fully understanding the seriousness of what we were doing, I purchased a little ring down at Jackson's drug store, and we announced our engagement.

And then, on April fifth, one month and three days after my sixteenth birthday, my cousin Alfred D. (We called him Afer-D) and I thumbed a ride to Rome Georgia and made our first attempt to join the Navy. Afer-D, who was bigger than I, went up to the counter first.

"Whirs yur birth certificate?" the recruiting officer growled.

"Ah... ah, I, ah" Afer-D blushed.

"Ya ain't no older than that little skinny fellow over thar," the guy with the bell-bottom britches hissed. "Get outta here."

We left.

However, unknown to Afer-D, I returned the next day with absolute proof that I was eighteen years old. The recruiting officer sat for a long time looking at the little Bible I brought as evidence. I had sat up late the night before copying the family record from my mother's big Bible in the front of the little book my parents had given me on my fifteenth birthday. The only change I made was the date of my own birth. Finally, when the officer looked up, I wished I could crawl under the rug.

"Pretty good forgery," the man laughed, holding the Bible up with the first page dog-eared and turned back. "Looks like you overlooked a little detail," he teased as he pointed to the publisher's notes, which read: "Schofield Facsimile Series No. 1, Copyright, 1901, renewed, 1917-1937 by Oxford University Press, New York, NY... Published July 17, 1938." I reached for the book and left the office without replying.

However, about a month later, after trying to join the Marine Corps, The Army, and the Army Air Corps, I decided to try the Navy again.

I was on my way to Knoxville. In those days, all young cowboys with a full set of strings on his guitar went to Knoxville, eventually.

The Greyhound bus I was on was going to Louisville. I learned at the Chattanooga station that the bus to Knoxville was late. With almost an hour to wait, and money in my pocket, I decided to look around town a little while I waited.

I walked up to the corner of Market Street and Cherry, I think, and was about to turn and go back the other way when I saw that wonderful inviting sign on a building across the street. "JOIN THE NAVY AND SEE THE WORLD."

I walked down to the crossing and was about to walk over when I noticed an old man standing slouched against the wall of a small building on the next block. This gave me a great idea. I had learned earlier that seventeen year olds could join the Navy with parental approval. This old man looked to me like the kind of old fellow who could use a couple of extra dollars.

"Want 't make five bucks easy?" I asked, as I approached.

"Doing what?"

"Go over there and tell them you're my daddy. Sign as my daddy so I can join the Navy."

"O. K. Where's the five bucks?"

I gave him the money and we walked over, both of us smiling from ear to ear.

However, my smile faded fast when the recruiting officer called the old man over and I realized that I had forgotten to tell the old fellow my name.

Sometime later our family went to the Church of God state convention at the Hemphill Avenue Church of God in Atlanta. Daddy said that I should take my guitar along... there would be lots of musicians there, and I might have a chance to play with some of them at one of the youths' functions during the week long activities.

Well, I had my chance, but it wasn't at one of the youth services which were held in the basement of the church. It happened during the long lunch break sometime about midweek. Lunch was, as usual, the traditional 'dinner on the ground', where a mountain of food was spread on a long line of picnic tables in a roped-off section of the parking lot. After eating, I had gone over to our car and was standing propped against the hood when a well-dressed lady came over, looked into the back of the car at my uncased guitar, and said,

"Nice guitar! You play?"

I was a little embarrassed. I knew who the lady was. I had seen her on stage with her husband and his brother several times since the convention started. She was Eva Mae LeFevre of the famous LeFevre trio.

"Sort of," I answered.

"I sort of sing a little," she said, mocking my terse answer, I thought. "I love guitar music," she continued. "Matter of fact I have a song that is just perfect for guitar... but, it has some minors, and the guy that plays guitar with us has a little trouble with minors. Get it out," she pointed at the guitar, "and I'll show you."

I got the old Silvertone out and stood looking at her for a moment, and she started to hum a tune... "Try G," she said.

I strummed a G chord and she started to sing and when she came to the minor chord she had mentioned, it was obvious from my experience of playing by ear... and when I made the switch to G-minor she smiled and said. "Come on... bring the guitar, I want you to show Alphus."

Well, as we walked across the tarmac and entered the church from the side door, I knew that Alphus LeFever knew more about minor chords than I ever would. I had listened to the famous LeFever trio on the radio many times, and I knew by then that Ms. Eva Mae LeFever was pulling my leg. And I rightly guessed that my daddy had had something to do with that charade.

We walked up on the podium and over to the big Baby Grand that stood adjacent the pulpit where I checked to see if my tuning was to standard. It was close.

The audience was moving around visiting each other and it seemed that everybody in the church was talking. And then, Eva Mae raised her hand and spoke into the mike.

"Listen up everybody. Listen up now." And the church became quite. "We have a new guitarist," she continued. "This," she said, holding her hand out to me palm up, "is Henderson Ponder. Henderson also will be attending BTS this term." The crowd cheered, and I was embarrassed again.

Then, Eva May motioned... I struck a G chord, and she started to sing. And suddenly, Alphus and Uras were beside her... the curtain behind us opened and the big church was filled with the sound of one of America's most popular gospel bands, augmented by the almost inaudible sound of my brand new forty nine dollar, curved top Silvertone guitar.

For those of you youngsters who do not remember the famous LeFever trio; Alphus LeFever composed one of World War II's most popular songs, 'Coming in on a Wing and a Prayer', and Eva Mae lived to become a popular regular with the Gaither gospel singers whom you have no doubt viewed on national television.

CHAPTER TEN

At summer's end I suddenly realized that it was time for me to go up to Sevierville Tennessee where I would start my first term at BTS. I had been working some during the summer at the little Blackwood grocery store on North Commerce, Street. And I was there on a Saturday morning placing apples, oranges, and other fruit in the fruit bins near the front door, when Mary Jim, Lou Cindy, and another girl came in. I glanced up and spoke to Mary Jim and noticed that the other girl, the one I had not seen before, had stepped behind a counter. I could see only part of her arm where she held onto the edge of the counter. Then, she turned and walked around the counter and looked over to where the other two girls and I stood... and believe me, I almost passed out.

"Dear Jesus!" I whispered under my breath. "Dear God, what a beautiful creature."

Mary Jim put her hand out in a gesture of recognition and said, "Henderson Ponder... Mary Frances Gilmer."

"Oh no!" I whispered to myself. "Not another Mary Frances." But, my mind was chanting. "Mary Frances, Mary Frances. Dear God, this is the one."

"Her nickname is Bunton" Lou Cindy said. "This is her birthday." And the beautiful creature stood there smiling at me as if she and I had some kind of great secret. My heart continued to pound as if it would burst and let that wonderful secret escape. And then, the beautiful stack of flesh and bones and like-silk curtain of auburn hair walked over to the fruit-bin, picked up a lemon and held it up to her cheek.

"Bunton!" I said. And I was thinking, "What kind of mother would call a beautiful creature like this Bunton?"

"Your birthday?"

"Yes. I'm fourteen today."

"Jesus," I thought, "If this isn't the cat's meow. All the pretty ones are either too old, or too young." And it was a fact. This beautiful creature was surely too young for a man almost seventeen years old, especially a man who would soon be in uniform serving his country.

Time finally came and Mary Frances... not the 'Bunton' one... the one with the ring, was at McGinnis drug store when the Greyhound bus came. Momma was there, and Daddy and Gertha and while Mary Frances and I said our goodbyes Daddy brought my big old trunk over and the bus man put it in the cargo compartment... and before I knew it, I was on my way to Sevierville Tennessee.

BTS was a new experience, as far as schools go. The entire student body was steeped in the unique religious doctrine of the Church of God. All faculty members were leaders in the church, and ascribed to the church doctrine which required that all functions commence with prayer. The Bible was read at each gathering and at some point during each class period. And, of course my long standing conviction that something was wrong with a doctrine that relegated so many classes of individuals to an eternity in Hell, for sometimes simply believing in an almost identical doctrine, was reignited. I wondered why the Christian faith leaned so heavily on the teachings of the Old Testament.

Example: Numbers 31:1-2 *And the Lord spake unto Moses saying, "Avenge the children of Israel of the Midianites: afterward shalt thou be gathered unto thy people." And Moses spake unto the people, saying, "Arm some of yourselves unto the war, and let them go against the Midianites, and avenge the Lord of Midian."*

Why I wondered, did the church put so much credence in the Old Testament which constantly claimed that God condoned... that God actually commanded, that people wage war against their neighbors; when in fact, Jesus who was the object of the Christian faith never encouraged violence in any form.

And of course, my doubts about the truth of the Christian faith grew and my concern about the commandment, *'Thou shalt not kill,'* left me in a state of total confusion.

However, I soon found other than my bewilderment about the church doctrine to occupy my mind. In exercising my right to select elective subjects for the school term, I had chosen Spanish as my preference in language. But when I wound up with a foreign student, a French lad who spoke with a heavy French accent as a roommate, I changed my mind.

My roommate was Jon Pierre Coldt, a French kid from Auxaire France. Jon Pierre's parents had left France a scant two weeks before the Germans breached the Maginot line. It seems that Monsieur Coldt had a real streak of luck. The company he worked for had a distribution center in Nashville.

Jon Pierre and I hit it off great from the beginning. In fact, we had some things, one in particular, in common. We both dreamed of a career in music... of course after we eliminated all those dirty Germans and Japanese.

I was fascinated with Jon Pierre's accent and determined to learn to speak French. Consequently, I changed my language course to French and started right away to pester Jon Pierre with questions about the language.

How do you say? "I've got to go to the bathroom," I would ask... and then spend hours whispering to myself, "Je dois aller aux toilettes". Or, "Will you have dinner with me" and Jon Pierre would answer, "Voulez-vous dîner avec moi".

On the weekend before Thanksgiving, Jon Pierre's parents came to Sevierville for an overnight visit. I was thrilled at the prospect of meeting them, especially his mother. Jon Pierre had talked incessantly about his mother...

about how she looked in the beautiful clothes Monsieur Coldt bought for her... about how sweet she smelled from the expensive perfumes she wore, and how she looked walking in the high-heel shoes she simply could not live without.

The morning before his parents arrived, I asked Jon Pierre what was the nicest thing a man could say to a French lady and spent much of the day whispering the phrase to myself.

When the Coldts arrived, Jon Pierre and I were waiting on the brick walk by a little patio just outside Robinson Hall. I watched as the big black car slid into the parking lot at the administration building and saw Monsieur Coldt get out and walk around to open the door for his wife.

Madame Coldt stepped out of the car, fluffing her cheveux (hair), as she started up the walk with Monsieur Coldt following. I could clearly hear the clacking sound of her high-heels from the little patio where Jon Pierre and I had moved just as the Coldts arrived.

Jon Pierre was smiling from ear to ear as he rushed down the hill to meet them... and I was almost as excited as he was. He had been right about his mother. She was indeed a beautiful lady.

When they came to the top of the hill and entered the patio, I stepped forward and put out my hand just as Jon Pierre started to introduce his mother to me. She offered her hand and I held it for a moment and bowed slightly at the waist. "Ah Mme Coldt. Voulez-vous coucher avec moi ce soir?"

Madame Coldts face turned almost as blue as the beautiful dress she wore. She looked at Jon Pierre and back at me.

"Vous êtes fou fou!" She screamed. "Vous êtes fou fou!"

At that moment, Monsieur Coldt arrived. He sized up the scene, listened for a moment to his wife's tirade, and started towards me with a flash of anger showing in the pools of blue that served as his eyes. Fortunately for me, Jon Pierre stepped into the fray and explained what had happened and why. Monsieur Coldt stopped, stood for a moment with a shy grin slightly moving his lips, and then started to laugh.

Madame Coldt stormed back down the walk, and I headed in the other direction to my room.

Sometime after lights out that night, Jon Pierre eased into the room. I lay quietly with my face to the wall and listened as he went to the bathroom, brushed his teeth, put on that silly little sleeping gown he wore, and climbed into the top bunk.

I could hear Jon Pierre laughing under his breath, and when I could stand it no longer, I ask. "What's so funny?"

"Nothing" he laughed.

"Well, what?"

"You asked my mother to sleep with you," he teased. "You asked her to sleep with you."

CHAPTER ELEVEN

That school term was probably one of the most troubling times of my young life. I was torn between the love of my guitar... of my dream of becoming a recognized country/western singer, and joining the armed forces and doing the very thing that had caused me to loose many long hours of sleep.

As far as the music was concerned, at least the music lessons... I found the routine to be less than satisfactory. My guitar instructor was Harold Cato from the well-known Cato family of Atlanta. His mastery of the guitar was somewhat short of impressive due to his physical impairment. However, his knowledge of the instrument and of music in general was phenomenal.

My other venture into the realm of music was voice lessons which were taught by another well known... B. O. Robinson, a composer whose name can be found in millions of church song books around the world.

The guitar lessons were somewhat boring. I had spent perhaps thousands of hours learning to play the instrument by ear, and sitting there on Mr. Cato's little stool trying to read the unfamiliar notes and find the proper string and fret was something just short of foolish. And the thing with Mr. B.O. Robinson was even worse.

However, my study of French, both in the classroom and under Jon Pierre's tutorial at night, brought me much satisfaction... after I settled the score with him about the 'Coucher avec moi,' episode.

All the other things about BTS simply bored me to death. English, math, science and Bible studies, along with prayer meetings, lectures, preaching and the constant sound of pianos, trumpets, drums, guitars and every other kind of musical instrument imaginable made for a truly boring time, in my opinion. I needed to get away from this beehive of sound and motion. I needed to find a way to get myself into some kind... any kind of military uniform, and find my way across the deep blue where I could finish off a few Krauts. And then, maybe I could go to Knoxville and talk to Mr. Blanchard again about my music career.

By this time, news of the war was a constant part of the daily routine. After supper each night, Jon Pierre and I would go to our room and turn on the radio. Between my questions, such as... Ce qui est dans la bouteille? And Jon Pierre's chiding about my hillbilly accent, we learned that the allied invasion of Italy which started September 3, had advanced up the boot-shaped peninsular to Viterbo north of Rome.

My thoughts were that our guys would jump all over Hitler's little bunch of bullies in France and chase them all the way back to Berlin before I could get there. And Jon Pierre worried that he would not be able to join because he was not legally a citizen. He wished that he could return to France and sign up with the Maquis.

Well, I didn't know much about that, but when my birthday approached, I packed my big old combination trunk and stand-up wardrobe and got on a Greyhound bus for Chattanooga and parts south. I had decided that there were more ways to skin a cat than one. I had decided that the best way to get by the recruiting officers and get myself in uniform was to register for the draft.

.

CHAPTER TWELVE

It's needless to say that my parents were somewhat upset when I dragged that old trunk through the front door. And if they had guessed my plan, I am sure that Daddy and I would have had a little conversation out behind the barn, as the saying goes.

However, being the loving and understanding parents they were, it was clear that they intended to give me ample time to explain my decision to leave BTS. Consequently, before giving them much chance to seek a definitive answer, I asked Daddy for the keys to his car, and drove back down town.

My plan was to go down to the Dixie five and dime at about closing time and drive Mary Frances home. However, as I drove up Commerce Street and came to the cross-walk at McGinnis drug store, I was distracted from my plan. Standing there waiting to cross the street was that pretty, too young to be so pretty girl... that other Mary Frances everybody called 'Bunton.'

I stopped at the pedestrian walk, rolled my window down and waited for her to cross, thinking that I would speak to her as she walked by. However, when she saw me watching, she turned her head and strolled by with an air of nonchalant condescension.

"Well," I whispered under my breath. "If the little squirt was old enough, I'd tell her a thing or two." But my eyes were locked on the beauty that strolled casually across my vision, and my heart fluttered a little within my chest. "Dang," my thoughts wandered on. "Why can't a pretty thing like that be a little older?"

I pulled over and parked just beyond the cross-walk, but after standing for a moment on the sidewalk in front of the Montgomery knitting mill, she turned the other way and walked down towards the theater. So consequently, by the time I made my way to the Dixie five and Dime, Mary Frances was already aboard the Victory bus heading out East Washington Street towards Highway 27. She was looking out the slightly foggy window and turned her head the same way Bunton had, when I approached.

However, during the next several weeks, Mary Frances and I got together several times... usually in the company of Mary Jim, Lou Cindy and others of the soda fountain bunch at Jackson's Drug store. And sometimes we would walk up and hang around at Willow Spring where the other girls would almost invariably look at Mary France's little engagement ring and tease us a little about our plan to get married.

Finally, I got up the nerve to go to the courthouse and register for the draft. And it was a matter of nerve, to be sure. The person in charge of the Chattooga County Selective Service board was Ms. Mae Earl Strange, a longtime resident of Berryton, Georgia. The image of that somewhat over-large woman was fresh in my mind, as I walked up the marble steps and entered the courthouse. Mae Earl Strange was well known to all the citizens of Berryton, Georgia and in my mind I was sure that she knew exactly when I was born. No doubt, I thought. Mae Earl Strange was sitting on the side of my mother's bed on the morning of March 2nd, 1927.

As it turned out, all the young men registering for the draft that week were born in 1926. And when Mae Earl came to me, she simply asked. "Date of birth?" and I answered the way the man before me had answered. "March 2nd."

"Henderson Ponder," she exclaimed. "Didn't you know you were supposed to register within two weeks of your birthday?"

When I stammered for an appropriate answer, she turned and started to thumb through a stack of papers. "Margie!" She yelled. "Bring me that list from the first week in March."

The lady Margie came in with the list and Mae Earl sat for a long time studying it, while I stood before her desk trying to calm the shaking of my hand. Finally, she wrote something on one of the pages, and looked up. "I'm putting you on the registry for March," she said. "Now, we'd better get you down to McPherson right away. How would Monday be?"

Boy that was great with me! If I could get away that soon, there would be little chance that Momma and Daddy would learn about my scheme in time to stop me.

So, when I got back home that morning, I told Momma that I wanted to go down and stay with my friend Leonard for a while at his parents' new home in Columbus, Georgia. Leonard had stayed at our house for weeks at a time over the past couple of years. I hoped that Momma and Daddy didn't know that Leonard was already in the army.

That Sunday, we went to Sunday school and church as usual, and the sermon that morning brought back an avalanche of doubt and bewilderment.

The sermon was taken from the book of Deuteronomy, and many of the verses the minister read were disturbing. For example, Chapter 32, verse 39-42. *"See now that I, even I, am He, and there is no God with me: I kill, and I make alive; I wound, and I heal; neither is there any that can deliver out of my hand For I lift up my hand to Heaven, and say, I live forever; If I whet my glittering sword, and mine hand take hold on judgment; I will render vengeance to mine enemies, and will reward them that shall devour flesh; and what with the blood of the slain and of the captives, from the beginning of revenges upon the enemy."*

"Is this the word of God," I thought, "or the ravings of some disgruntled Jew longing for revenge against the Arabs, who even then sought to destroy the Jewish nation?"

Is this really God,   Is this God's way of speaking to me… of telling me that it is O.K. to kill a few Krauts?   If that was true, I wondered… what about *'Thou shalt not kill?'*   What about what the preacher always said about those who break God's commandments going to Hell?

But then, what about, "I guess, a fellow has to do what a fellow has to do?"

CHAPTER THIRTEEN

At Fort McPherson I entered my preference for the Army Air Force on one of the forms they gave us. But after the physical, which included an eye examination, I was assigned to the group which was headed to the infantry training center at Camp Blanding Florida.

At this time, I wish to point out that details about my training phase and the balance of my first enlistment in the army have been chronicled in a trilogy of books titled "Mesha," "San Mario Island," and "Judische Jade." These works are pseudo-fictional novels laced with flash-back memories of some of the events that befell me during that time. They detail in a crude fashion, many of the events that... when mingled with the doubts and confusion suffered during my youth, caused me to miss many of the pleasures enjoyed by those who believe and trust in the reality of God.

Consequently, since I do not wish to re-hash those events, I will skip forward... hoping that you might read the novels mentioned above, and especially the epilog and author's notes therein.

However, there is one event that happened during that time which I wish to present. It is something that happened immediately after my team landed in the European war zone.

When our little Victory ship arrived at Le Havre, France, the harbor was cluttered with sunken ships and broken airplanes. The city of Le Havre, at least the part we were able to see near the harbor, was a pile of bricks and mortar. A number of American and British ships, some very large ones, were standing at moorings next to large floating docks, and the spaces between them and the shore were laced with flimsy looking floating piers or walkways. Our little tub found a place and snuggled up to one of the contraptions, and when it was time for us to disembark we climbed down rope netting and waddled up one of the shaky little things with all our gear... duffle, weapons, extra shoes, blankets, gas masks, and a few chocolate bars.

There were about thirty or thirty-two men left in our forty- eight man team, the 117 Army Operations Team. Several had washed out at the special ops' training center near Stark Florida, and a couple had been pulled out at Kilmer for reassignment. But, thirty or thirty-two was all we needed. We were the toughest bunch of fellows in the world, and our officers were the smartest. If you didn't know that, all you had to do was to ask.

However, those Einsteins with the shiny little bars had forgotten to arrange for our transport north to the railhead where we were to board a train for Namur Belgium. It had already been decided that the 117th would go to Namur, where the team would be decommissioned (as they say in the army) and parceled out to first army units already in Germany.

It was almost dark when old super brain, Major Turner, figured out that one had to flash his brass and beat his chest to get the attention of those six-by-six jockeys, and finally we were allowed to sit on ammo boxes on three noisy tarp covered trucks.

When we arrived at the railhead it was totally dark. But some torches and campfires allowed us to see what looked like a very long train with snuggly warm-looking passenger cars much like the ones we had ridden when we went from Stark Florida to Camp Picket Virginia. However, the big train lost all appeal when we spotted the huge field mess the QM had established in the pine woods beyond the tracks. As we entered the mess area it was obvious that those Quarter Master boys had brought their bed warmers. Many of the tents we passed were lighted with lanterns or other means, and where the tent flaps were ajar, the silhouette of some bodies that didn't look exactly like those boys serving the grub could be seen.

The beans, fried cabbage, and cornbread was pretty good, but before we could gobble it down that beautiful warm passenger train tooted its horn and started to puff off up the tracks.

"That's all right. There's another train down the tracks." Somebody yelled. But when we were through eating and made our way back to the tracks, the train we found standing there was certainly not the Seaboard Express. In fact it could hardly even be called a freight train, because most of the cars were not standard freight cars... they were actually cobbled up wood and scrap metal boxes sitting on what appeared to have been freight train flat cars. In fact they were what the Germans referred to as "Jüde Wagons"

It was obvious that some remodeling had been done after the Krauts pawned them to Patton's boys. The doors had been removed and heavy canvas had been fastened across the front end of each of the cars. However, there was no means to heat the things except for a little coal heater that had been placed in the forward end near the leading wall. But there was no coal.

As we selected one of the cars and started to load our gear aboard, the wind started to blow and a light sprinkle of misty rain warned us that the trip in this full-of-holes contraption was not going to be a pleasant one. But there was nothing else to do but climb aboard.

I admit that at that time I knew little to nothing about the plight of the Jews in Europe, and I am sure that most of you were in the same boat. Looking back at that time it seems to me that the Jewish problem, as Heinrich Himmler would have said, was the best kept secret in the world. Oh... it's true that Gabriel Heater might have mentioned something about the Jews on the radio, but I don't think most people knew very much about what was going on.

OK, back to the train ride. I seem to be wandering all over the place with this piece.

Back to the train ride is a good way to put it. I go back there more often than I have admitted. To say that that night and most of the next day was a miserable time in my life is a colossal understatement. We sat there in that contraption huddled together as close as young men like to sit and listened to our teeth chatter. The mist of rain turned to snow, and the fact that the front of the car was covered with tarp made little difference. It's amazing how wind and snow can crawl through even the bullet holes in a piece of tin and cover an unlaced boot. And it is no wonder that the men sitting towards the back of that " Jüde Wagon" were almost frozen into popsicles before we got to Namur.

In reflecting back on that time it's almost laughable that I should have been so miserable. I knew where I was going. I knew, or at least I hoped that the next day I would have a hot meal and a warm place to sleep. I knew that my commanding officer could tell that train driver where to go and when to stop. I could see that the blood on the floor of that old forty-and-eight was not mine or that of one of my loved ones. I could see that it had dried and was almost unnoticeable.

But what about the ones before me? What about the Jews... men, women, children, and babies. They had only rumor and innuendo to point the way to their destiny. They could not hope for a good hot meal and a warm place to sleep. They had committed the unforgivable sin. They had been born a Jew. How dare that they should live in the same world with Adolph, Herman, and Eva Braun.

They were no doubt related to... or descendants of somebody who was related to that fellow, what's his name? Something like, Jessie. You know that guy who claimed he was some kind of big shot from Mars or something. Yeh! I know. That fellow my mother used to tell me about. "Jesus".

CHPTER FOURTEEN

At the end of my first tour of duty, I returned to Paris France where I was given extra points for service within an enemy occupied territory and scheduled for repatriation. However, when our group stopped for a couple of days in Bremen Germany on our way to Bremerhaven, the port of deportation, I learned that one could re-enlist and remain overseas. And being the fool that I am, I made my way back to Paris and re-upped for a second term.

I was sent to Valkenburg, Holland where I received another job for which I was not qualified... that of tracking MIA's for Graves Registration. I arrived in Valkenburg late in the afternoon and did not meet the commanding officer until the next morning when he sent for me to come upstairs to his office.

After a long conversation wherein the C.O. explained some things about my new line of work, he said he wanted to show me something, and we went outside and drove a short distance out of town.

.

Alongside a dirt road, we got out of the Jeep and walked across a field to a group of men who were working near a long ditch, or pit, which had been unearthed. Standing in the ditch were a number of German prisoners-of-war who were lifting bodies out of the dirt and laying them in a neat row beside the ditch.

It is impossible to see faces in this shot, but you can bet that all the people in that ditch had faces... at least, before the Germans put them there.

Many of the bodies in the ditch held a handful of hair and had mouths full of dirt, indicating that they had been buried alive. Many were the bodies of very small children... infants who were guilty of nothing but being born a Jew.

I could not believe my eyes. I could not, and I still can't understand how any human being could murder innocent babies. And I can never understand how a God fearing nation such as ours has come to condone the killing of millions of babies in the name of a woman's right to choose. Surely, there are certain exceptions wherein an abortion might be performed. For example, in the case of rape it is plain that the women had no right to choose... however, others are not deprived of such right; there is a thing called, "abstinence". And with today's technologies in contraception, one does not even have to adhere to that method. Other exceptions surely are condonable. If a woman's life is severely threatened, there obviously should be consideration.

I do not condemn the German citizens who did not speak out against the atrocities mentioned above... or those who drove the bulldozers and participated in the act. They had no right to oppose their leaders, nor did they possess the wonderful means of a secret ballot to disenfranchise them.

It is said that the Germans exterminated over six million Jews during the war. I read somewhere that there have been over twenty eight million innocent little babies murdered in the United States since the passing of Row-V-Wade.

CHAPER FIFTEEN

During the remainder of my stay overseas, due to my job as an investigator with Graves Registration, I was afforded travel throughout Western Europe, and parts of North Africa.

After working throughout most of Holland, parts of Germany and Belgian, we moved our headquarters to Troyes France. And shortly thereafter I left Troyes in a jeep with two other young men to investigate a report that an army officer had been found and buried in a small village cemetery near the little village of Champenone.

There was nothing strange that the officer had been buried in a local civilian cemetery, this was a common practice. However, the location of the village was in the vicinity where a certain army Major had gone missing.

The three of us in the jeep were about the same age, and although we were of different ethnicity and background, we were creatures of the same hue... our interests could be described in three words... wine, women, and song.

The young man driving the jeep was a first generation Polish American who had joined the army only about six months earlier. We called him "Shaky". The interpreter was Jacque Piaf, a young man from Chalon-sur-Saone France.

The village we were to visit was very close to another village where Jacque was born. As it turned out, Jacque's aunt Rosa Piaf still lived in the village. As a matter of fact, she was the Burgomaster (Mayor). Consequently, Jacque asked if we could go by and visit his aunt... and I was glad when I was introduced to Madame Piaf and her lovely daughter Monique.

Monique and I were quick to size each other up and just as quickly found an excuse to examine the flowers in Madame Piaf's garden.

Finally, much too soon, Jacque, knowing that it was time for us to go, came outside and announced that Aunt Rose wanted us to return to her house for lunch. My reply to that was what you might already have guessed... only if Monique could ride with us.

As soon as Madame Piaf agreed, we piled into the jeep and started down the graveled road. Shaky and Jacque naturally sat in the front seat, and I made sure that Monique had a comfortable place next to me in the back.

Then the game began, a game that only Shaky and Jacque understood. I could hear Jacque shout. "Come on Shaky! Make it slide." And Shaky would turn the wheel from side to side and cause the little jeep to slide on the loose graveled road. "Come on Shaky! Make it slide".

Suddenly, the road forked and Shaky first turned to the right lane and then back to the left. I could see that the jeep was skidding sideways into a rather thick hedge that separated the confluence of the road and a stone house. The house was slightly lower than the road and shielded by a tall plank fence which gave the occupants a modicum of privacy and perhaps the allusion of safety.

I grabbed the girl's arm and screamed, "Sauter!" but there was no time to jump... we were already airborne. The world seemed to change to a slow motion mode, and I could see the fence coming at us and the jeep following. The jeep apparently turned and hit the fence with its front bumper a split second before I reached it.

I opened my eyes and realized that my face was on the ground. I raised my head, listened, and wondered if I could not hear because I was dead. And then I heard the wheels of the jeep turning and felt the trickle of gas hitting my leg. I smelled the gas and realized that Monique was lying on top of me.

"Get off!" I almost screamed. "Get off! The gas, the gas," and then I realized that she didn't understand me. "Descendez! J'ai presque crié. Descendez! Le gaz, legaz! J'ai presque crié. Descendez! Le gaz, legaz," I repeated in my hastily half learned French, and the girl started to crawl forward. I felt her slide forward and turned slightly on my side and realized that the jeep was on top of us. However, fortunately we were not pinned in. We were lying under the jeep in the only place a body could lie without being crushed. We were lying on the ground directly under the front seat of the jeep. Apparently, the front bumper of the jeep had struck the side of the rock building about six feet from the ground and slid straight down the wall, crushing the windshield and pressing the steering wheel slightly down, leaving the cavity where we lay.

When we were safely out from under the jeep, I heard the sound of the gasoline running into a large tin bucket. Some enterprising citizen had thought to catch and preserve the almost impossible to get treasure.

Almost immediately, a passing motorist, an army Captain and two enlisted men stopped to see what had happened. After learning that Jacque, Shaky, and I were only scratched and bruised, and that Monique had survived with only a bruised and slightly fractured shoulder blade, we were driven back to a small civilian medical clinic in Jacque's and Madame Piaf's home village.

After we were examined and dismissed by the local doctor, the Captain insisted that he be allowed to drive us back to Troyes. But I just as vehemently insisted on staying long enough to learn how badly Monique was hurt. Then, shortly after Madame Piaf came out of Monique's room, paused momentarily to give me a hard and resentful look, I was allowed to go in and see the girl.

Three days later I drove back to Monique's home and strangely enough was pleasantly greeted by the lady Burgomaster. Monique and I walked out to a small nearby park and sat for a long time talking as best we could with my faulty French. And it was there that I learned that Madame Piaf was reluctant to allow Monique to go with us that day.

She only relented because Jacque was the son of her husband's brother. And it was there that I learned that the Madame had walked across the park to the village church and knelt, and was in fact praying for our safe journey at the very moment we went over the hedge.

Now! Here is the strange part of my story. About a week later I received a letter from my mother and learned, after, figuring the difference in the time zones in France and Summerville Georgia, that at the moment we were driving along that dirt road... at the moment Jacque was teasing Shaky to "Come on Shaky! Make it slide" (It was about 5:25 a.m. in Summerville), my little sister rushed into our parents room crying. She had dreamed that something horrible was about to happen to me and at the very moment we crashed into the old stone house in that little village in France, my parents also were on their knees in Summerville, Georgia praying for me.

CHAPTER SIXTEEN

Over the next several months, I traveled extensively throughout France and made additional forays back into Holland, Germany and Belgium. Then I flew into Gibraltar from where I made my second and third entries into Spain and over the straights to North Africa. Finally, I made my way back to Paris for a little R and R before traveling to Bremerhaven Germany and the trip home.

At some time during that period, Mary Frances... the one with the ring, decided our childish decision to become engaged wasn't such a good idea after all. Consequently, I received a letter telling that my little ring would be in a drawer waiting when I got home.

Well, I honestly can't say that that was a disappointment to me at the time. As a matter of fact, although she was really a very pretty girl, I had often had to get her picture out of my wallet in order to conjure up an image of her. And, to tell the truth, I actually thought more often of that other cute little Mary Frances... the one they called 'Bunton'. However, there were many things happening in my life at that time to keep my mind from 'cute little girls' back home.

The work I was doing brought me to view death in all its ugly forms... often adding to the confusion, and doubt that had fermented within my mind over the years of my youth.

Although it was not my charge to handle the bodies we collected, it was often necessary for me to accompany a DT (disinterment team) to the gravesite or other location where a body was found. And, sometimes I would help move a corpse to a better position for the medics to perform the forensics necessary for identification.

On one occasion, I was sent to investigate the site of a downed fighter plane in an effort to determine what had happened to the pilot who was reported missing in action.

At the scene, I asked the interpreter to go around to several houses in the vicinity and ask if anybody was present when the crash occurred. And, very soon we had a couple of dozen people on hand, all talking at the same time. It seemed that everybody present knew what had happened to the pilot... but it was soon evident that we were getting several different scenarios of the event.

Finally, the interpreter and I went back to the jeep and asked the driver to drive into the village and find the Catholic Church. I had long since learned that in countries like France, the local priest is the best source of information related to birth, death, and a host of other matters.

When we found the church and were cordially invited into the priests' office, we were offered the traditional glass of wine, which we accepted graciously. To do otherwise, we knew would be taken as an insult and render our visit worthless.

After the wine and pleasantries, the priest called in an altar boy and sent for a man whom he said 'knew the whole story.' And, it was indeed a story.

According to our informant, a group of S.S. was stationed in the village at the time of the crash, and when news that a U. S. fighter plane had crashed in a field outside the village, the group commander ordered his men out to investigate the scene. "Upon arriving," the informant continued... "the men, seeing that the pilot's body was severely torn and somewhat scattered over the ground, proceeded to collect body parts and feed them to their dogs."

After further investigation to determine the identity of the S.S officer guilty of the crime, my report as required, was forwarded to the proper authorities at Nuremberg. However, I was never to learn if the guilty men were ever captured and punished for the dastardly crime.

There were many other things that happened during that time that served to augment my doubts that the preacher at the Berryton Church of God had been truly honest about God's vengeance towards those who transgressed against his commandments. After all, it appeared that God condoned many of man's transgressions, as indicated in the book of Deuteronomy, and other scripture throughout the Old

Testament. Maybe the Germans who committed the crime at the scene of the plane crash would not go to Hell for their sins. If they could escape the wrath of the war crimes commission, maybe they were assured a reward in Heaven for good things they were sure to have done in life. Maybe my own transgressions, I surmised, will be forgiven.

CHAPTER SEVENTEEN

Finally, I was going home. Finally, I was aboard a large ship in a big room the Navy calls a hole and on my way home.

After what seemed like an eternity of climbing up to the fourth tier of bunks and climbing down again for yet another climb up a mountainous expanse of metal stairs known as ladders for what the navy called chow... our ship finally entered the welcomed waters of New York harbor.

As soon as we arrived at Camp Kilmer New Jersey and were settled into our 'home for a day', I called my friend Mario over the river in New York City. I had learned earlier that he had already returned home from overseas. Mario set in right away for me to come over to the city. We had not seen each other for some time now, and he said he was anxious to talk to me about his plan for me to work for his family after my discharge from the army.

Well, in the first place, I didn't have time to go to New York City. We had been told that we would be leaving in the morning for Fort Brag, North Carolina where we would muster out of the army. And, I knew that my first trip would not be to

New York City. My first trip would be to Summerville, Georgia where I would be reunited with my family, and maybe look up that little gal, Bunton.

But, Mario would not give up. He would finally come to Summerville and convince me to give the Big Apple a try.

However, that is really beside the point. Mario and the eye-opening lessons I would learn about his family and the business they carried on has little bearing on the tenets of this work. Consequently, let me tell you about my arrival home.

It's needless to say that my parents were elated when I threw my duffel bag into the living room at 310 South Edmonson Street that afternoon. I had not made them aware of my return to the U. S. and my discharge from the army.

It was almost five o'clock in the afternoon, and after a few hugs and a piece of Momma's apple pie, I asked if they would mind if I went down town before the stores closed.

Daddy gave me his keys and playfully pushed me towards the door. "Better hurry back," he teased, "Momma's 'bout to fry up some chicken."

I did hurry back. I stopped and looked in at Jackson's drug store, and at McGinnis's... and then drove up to the Pennville skating rink. But nobody I saw looked like the little auburn-haired gal that had occupied a special place in my memory for so long. I went back home disappointed, and helped my daddy with the fried chicken.

The next morning I walked over to the jobsite where Daddy was helping to build a warehouse at the cotton mill, and learned from the job foreman that I could go to work there, if I wanted to. However, I wasn't ready quite yet to start to work. I had to sort things out in my mind first. I had thought that I might go back up to Knoxville and talk to Mr. Blanchard again about a job with one of the country music groups he managed. He had told me earlier, when I was in school at BTS in Sevierville, that I should finish my schooling first, and then come to see him. Well, I hadn't finished school, but I had been half way around the world, and I certainly had learned a thing or two.

I got Daddy's car, drove up town and visited a few places where I used to hang out. I stopped at the pool room on East Washington, and went back to Jackson's where I sat alone at the fountain over a cherry coke and a flood of memories.

Just as I was leaving Jackson's, Lou Cindy and Vickie Tate came in the store and sat down in a booth. I walked over and ask, "Seen Mary Jim?"

"Mary Jim's in Florida." Vickie said. "She got married."

"Oh! I didn't know Leonard was back, yet."

"She didn't marry Leonard." Lou Cindy said. "I think Leonard went home. He lives in Columbus, you know."

"Well," I ventured. "What about that girl, uh Bunton somebody. She still around?"

"Yeah, uh Bunton." Vickie laughed. "Pretty thing's still around. She lives up at Dickeyville."

"Dickeyville?" I asked. I knew where Pennville was, but I had never heard of Dickeyville. "Where's that?"

"This side of Trion and that side of Pennville... you know, up where preacher Harold built that new theater?"

I started to walk towards the door, stopping for a moment to look back at the empty line of stools and the booth where the two girls sat. I had never seen the fountain at Jackson's drug store look so empty at this time of the day.

"Better hurry," Vickie laughed. "Better hurry. Pretty girl, uh, Bunton might get away."

CHAPTER EIGHTEEN

The next morning I went back to town and bought a used car at the Ford place. It was a 1941 Ford convertible... a red and white affair with white leather upholstery. It wasn't exactly what I wanted, but the fact was, it was the best I could afford.

That afternoon I drove down to Berryton and visited the Freemans. Tommy had just returned home from the army, and he wanted me to play with their band... the Southern Swing Boys. It seemed that he had been saddled with playing rhythm guitar with the band at the local square-dance in a place called the "Hanger." And of course, playing rhythm guitar for a square-dance is nothing but hard work.

However, I agreed to relieve him if his big brother Sammy, liked the idea. Sammy was the fiddler and the manager of the band. But, as I expected, he didn't like the idea of paying another rhythm man since Tommy was in the family. But Tommy insisted that he be relived from playing at least half of the normal sets, and Sammy reluctantly made me an offer.

Although I hated square-dance music, I was rather glad to accept the offer. Even if the job was for only two or three days a week, the pay was almost as much as the amount the foreman at Daddy's job had offered me for a forty hour week.

Another decision I made that week would give me some satisfaction and help to take my mind off the things I had been trying so hard to forget for so long. On Wednesday I ran into Joe Eleam at the poolroom. Joe told me that he was taking flying lessons at a little dirt field north of Trion. He said that I could sign up at the field and that the G. I. Bill would pay all the expense.

Well, it didn't take me long to drive up to the airfield and sign up for the private pilot's course. It's needless to say that my mother and daddy were not too happy about that.

After my first flying lesson on Friday of that week, and my fist Saturday night at the Hanger, Daddy said that it was time for me to get back into church. So, on Sunday morning I got into the back seat of Daddy's car and rode the two and a half blocks to the Summerville Church of God on Bellah Avenue.

The sermon that morning was just about what I expected. "Thou shalt not this, and thou shalt not that... and if you don't do what the book says, you're going to Hell."

As you might have guessed, I simply closed my mind to all that. I just sat there in church that morning and tried to think back on more pleasant things. I remembered the time Alfer D and I spent the day swinging on the old vine that hung

83

from the top of a big hickory tree over Raccoon creek. And I remembered the day just before I left for my short stay at BTS, when Mary Jim and Lou Cindy came into the little grocery store where I worked with that cute little girl, Bunton. And, I determined that I would look her up and find out why she seemed to avoid me since my returning home.

Consequently, I drove around town the next day looking for her. And finally late in the afternoon, I stopped at the Pennville skating rink and found her. She was out on the floor making beautiful circles, and looking as if she were flying through a fluffy white cumulus cloud the way I had done in the old J-3 cub the day before.

I stood at the rail and watched her for a long time, and then she glided over to a bench near where I stood and sat for a moment adjusting her skates.

I moved over and stood behind her. "I've been looking for you," I said.

She looked around. "Oh! Do I know you?"

"We met down at the little grocery store on Commerce Street in Summerville," I said.

"Oh! I don't remember,"

"You were with Mary Jim and Lou Cindy," I countered.

"Oh! Mary Jim... I think she got married, moved down to Florida. That the one?"

"Yeah!"

She stood up and straightened her skirt. "Nice meeting you," she smiled as she pushed off and started another spin around the rink. And then, she stopped at another bench on the other side, removed her skates and left the rink with a boy I had never seen before.

CHAPTER NINETEEN

Today is December 21st, 2012 and I sit here at Bunton's graveside in the cemetery at Summerville, Georgia. It is our 65th wedding anniversary and she has lain here a total of 74 days. My heart is heavy with grief and my mind is filled with memories of the wonderful times we had together.

I vividly remember the day I finally got to sit down with her and talk. It was on a Sunday afternoon in the spring of 1947, shortly after I returned from New York City. I dove up to her house in Pennville, and asked the lady who came to the door. "Is Frances home?"

"Yes!" She said, as she turned and yelled back into the front room... "Bunton!"

Bunton came to the door. "Hi!" She said, after the lady went inside and closed the door. "I've been expecting you. How did you know where I live?"

"Well," I said. "Finding people is what I've been doing for a living the last couple of years. Are you about ready to sit down and talk to me?"

"Why not?" She teased. "Sit and talk!" she motioned towards the swing, and we walked over and sat down.

"Well," she said. "Talk!"

"Uh... Well," I stammered. "I've been gone since shortly after we met. I've been overseas, and I've... well, I've been thinking about you a lot."

"Oh!" She said.

"Well," I continued, "I guess I figured that you're just about old enough now... well, you know? Uh, about old enough to hang around with a fellow like me."

"Oh!" She countered. "Think I might have something to say about that?"

"Not a word." I said as I got up and walked to the edge of the porch. "Just go in there and put on your prettiest dress, powder your nose and I'll pick you up at seven thirty."

At seven thirty I was there and she was sitting in the swing on the front porch looking like a movie star. "Damn," I said under my breath. As I took her by the arm and we walked to the car, I said casually, "You look pretty good for a little girl."

We drove around for a while and talked small talk. She asked what I was planning to do now that I was a civilian again... and I said, "Well, right now I don't really know. For the time being, I'm working with the Southern Swing Boys down at the Hanger."

"Sounds like a great occupation," she teased. "When do you plan to get a regular job?"

"You mean, like work?"

She laughed and pulled the visor down to look at herself in the mirror just as I turned in at the Moonlight drive-in theater.

I paid the fee, found an empty slot in a good location for both watching the movie and snuggling up, if the chance occurred... and then when the speaker was properly adjusted, I turned to her and said. "Stop messing around with your face. If you get any prettier, I'm likely to have a heart attack."

Today as I sit here and look at this precious mound of dirt, I remember that night as if it were only yesterday.

And, although there were many wonderful days and nights between that day and the day we were married... that day still brings a flutter to my heart.

When she agreed to marry me, after considerable persuasion on my part, we made absolutely no plans other than to go somewhere and get married. The next day after she agreed, I asked Bob, her father to meet at the courthouse and sign the papers, because she was only seventeen years old. And, it's needless to say that I was surprised when he agreed.

The day after acquiring the marriage license, I got Leonard, and that girl (Nancy, or something) in the car and drove up to Bunton's house.

She was out of the house and in the car almost before I could stop the thing, and, we were on our way to LaFayette, Georgia where a preacher I knew had moved. We drove up to the preacher's house and I got out and went to the door. I had not called the man in advance. He came to the door, recognized me and put out his hand. "Henderson! I heard you were back. How are things going?"

"Great," I said. "Got a little job for you," I continued. "Little gal out there and me want to get married. We wondered if you'd say the proper words for us." I paused.

"Gee Henderson, I'm sorry. I've got a little problem myself today. My wife's about to have a baby, and we were just about ready to go to the hospital."

"Oh, I'm sorry... I mean congratulations." I said. "We'll just run back down to Trion."

"Yeah," he said, as I turned and walked back down the walk to the car... "And, congratulations to you as well."

When we got to Trion I drove up to the Trion Church of God and walked up the path to the door. I could tell by the number of cars parked in the parking area that someone was inside. And they were... about twenty people including the preacher and his wife were inside working to decorate the church for Christmas. The preacher was up on a ladder stringing lights around a large fir tree.

"What can I do for you?" he said, as I walked up and stood looking up at the tree.

"Looking for somebody to perform a wedding ceremony," I said. "We went up to preacher Waite's at LaFayette, but his wife's having a baby."

"Oh! Well, I guess we could do it here. You ready now?"

"Yeah! I'll get them in."

When we got inside the church, everybody except the preacher was sitting down on the first two rows of benches on the left side of the church. One of the ladies got up and went to the piano, and the preacher's wife came to meet us near the back of the church. She sorted us out and marched us to the front of the church and told us where to stand. And then, she led Leonard and Bunton to the back of the church and when the lady at the piano started to play the wedding march, she had Leonard escort Bunton up to stand by me.

The preacher stood before us and chanted the verses from a little book he held in his hand, and we made our vows, and Leonard proffered the little ring I had bought at Jackson's drug store (the new ring), and within ten minutes we were back in the car and headed back to Summerville.

CHAPTER TWENTY

As I mentioned earlier, our marriage was not the best planned affair. Both of our families learned about it only days before the event. As a matter of fact, I had not even met Bunton's grandmother 'Mamaw'... and my parents had only been hastily introduced to Bunton when we stopped by our house to pick up my camera one afternoon.

Of course, my mother had already checked up on the Gilmer family. My aunt Anna Bell knew the family, and she surmised that even if they were Baptists, they were a pretty good lot. Consequently, I was not surprised when, after supper on our first night together at my parents' house, Daddy asked,

"Where do you go to church?"

Bunton looked a little embarrassed. "My family goes to the South Summerville Baptist church, but I belong at the Pennville Gospel Tabernacle."

"Oh!" Daddy said. "That a Baptist church?"

"Not exactly," she said, looking at me as if I could answer the query. "It's sort of interdenominational."

Momma spoke up. "We'll take you to a real church Sunday," she smiled.

Well, I had already decided long ago that people were not going to Hell simply because they were Baptist. As a matter of fact, I had just about come to the conclusion that there was no such thing as Hell, except the Hell that people created themselves. What about the situation that had sucked the big part of the world into World War II? If there was ever a Hell on earth, that was surely the biggest one. And one could not surmise that the entire fault for that debacle should lie on the back of Hitler. He was a mean bugger, to be sure, but a lot had happened prior to the onset of the Nazi era to give the Hitlers of the world the excuse they sought.

As these thoughts coursed through my mind, I heard Daddy clear his throat, and knew immediately what was about to happen. At our house, the Bible was read and a prayer said before anybody went to bed. Daddy said!

"Well, get the Bible, Emmie."

Momma went to the bookshelf and brought the Bible back and sat back down on the couch by Daddy. Bunton looked over at me and smiled.

Momma started to read at Matthew 5:43 *"You have heard that it was said, 'You shall love your neighbor and hate your enemy.' But I say to you, Love your enemies and pray for those who persecute you, so that you may be sons of your*

Father who is in heaven. For he makes his sun rise on the evil and on the good and sends rain on the just and on the unjust. For if you love those who love you, what reward do you have? Do not even the tax collectors do the same? And if you greet only your brothers, what more are you doing than others? Do not even the Gentiles do the same? You therefore must be perfect, as your heavenly Father is perfect.

Then she turned to Matthew 6:24*"No one can serve two masters, for either he will hate the one and love the other, or he will be devoted to the one and despise the other. You cannot serve God and money. "Therefore I tell you, do not be anxious about your life, what you will eat or what you will drink, nor about your body, what you will put on. Is not life more than food and the body more than clothing?*

And then she finished with *John 14:21 "Whoever has my commandments and keeps them, he it is who loves me. And he who loves me will be loved by my Father, and I will love him and manifest myself to him." Judas (not Iscariot) said to him, "Lord, how is it that you will manifest yourself to us, and not to the world?" Jesus answered him, "If anyone loves me, he will keep my word, and my Father will love him, and we will come to him and make our home with him. Whoever does not love me does not keep my words. And the word that you hear is not mine but the Father's who sent me.*

When she had finished, Daddy cleared his throat and said, "Amen... Now, let's pray."

Momma and Daddy got down on their knees, and I sat forward in my chair and bowed my head. I had stopped kneeling at the family prayer sessions when I came home from the army. I knew that my parents were gravely disappointed in me, but they had not mentioned my disrespect, as Momma would have put it.

I glanced over and Bunton was kneeling before her chair. And then, as Daddy started to pray I noticed that her lips were moving and the expression on her face was one of deep concern. I felt almost ashamed that I too was not on my knees.

CHAPTER TWENTY ONE

On Friday afternoon that week, I called Tommy and told him I would not be at the square-dance that night, and we went up to the Moonlight drive-in theater and watched 'The Road to Morocco'. Then, on Saturday I asked Bunton if she wanted to go to the dance with me. She said she did not.

"I've heard enough about that place." She said. And I was glad she didn't want to go.

On Sunday morning, as Momma had promised, we went to church at the Summerville Church of God. Bunton and I went to the young singles' class where I normally attended. Ms. Young asked me to introduce my new friend, and everybody laughed... they all knew that Bunton and I were married.

I stood up and gestured toward Bunton with my left hand. "This ugly gal," I smiled, "is Bunton. I picked her up at the skating rink last week, and can't seem to get rid of her." Everybody laughed again.

"Be glad to take her off your hands." Charles Mason whispered.

"Okay, boys," Ms. Young said, "None of that," she turned to Bunton. "We're very proud to have you with us Bunton. I'm sure that isn't your real name, but it's very pretty. You belong to church anywhere?" Bunton sort of blushed.

"Yes, I belong at the Pennsville Gospel Tabernacle."

"Well... now that you're a member of the Ponder family, we hope you'll decide to be one of our church family too." She turned to the class.

"Turn to John 1 through 17... Please read for us, Ann."

Ann Oglesby stood up and read. *In the beginning was the Word, and the Word was with God, and the Word was God. The same was in the beginning with God. All things were made by him; and without him was not anything made that was made. In him was life; and the life was the light of men. And the light shineth in darkness; and the darkness comprehended it not. There was a man sent from God, whose name was John. The same came for a witness, to bear witness of the Light that all men through Him might believe. He was not that Light, but was sent to bear witness of that Light. That was the true Light, which lighteth every man that cometh into the world. He was in the world, and the world was made by Him, and the world knew Him not. He came unto his own, and His own received Him not. But as many as received Him, to them gave He power to become the sons of God, even to them that believe on His name: Which were born, not of blood, nor of the will of the flesh, nor of the will of man, but of God. And the Word was made flesh, and dwelt among us, (and we beheld his glory, the glory as of the only begotten of the*

Father,) full of grace and truth. John bare witness of Him, and cried, saying, this was He of whom I spake, He that cometh after me is preferred before me: for He was before me. And of his fullness have all we received, and grace for grace. For the law was given by Moses, but grace and truth came by Jesus Christ."

"Who wants to comment on that?" Ms. Young asked. She looked around the room, but nobody moved. She turned and looked at Bunton.

"I think," Bunton said, "that the prophet John was saying that, although the people of that time had the word of God... that they didn't understand the true meaning of God's purpose until Christ came to earth."

"Well!" Ms. Young said. "That's a good way to put it. Thank you Mrs. Ponder... uh, Bunton. Anybody else want to comment?"

When nobody spoke up, she folded her Bible and sat down and started to talk to one of the girls, and suddenly everybody in the room was talking.

That night I told Momma that we were going to skip the evening service, and we drove down to Rome and ate at the Partridge, a restaurant on Broad Street.

When we were through eating, Bunton sat back, looking a little embarrassed. "I want to ask you to do something for me." She said.

"Anything you want!" I ventured. I knew that there was nothing she could ask that I would not do.

"I want to ask you not to work at that square dance," she almost whispered. "I know that's asking a lot. I know how much you love to play music, and I really love to hear you play... but, please don't go down there anymore. Please?"

Well, she really didn't know how much she was asking of me. Without the square dance, there was no other venue for me... no other place where I could play the guitar and live in Summerville, Georgia. And, although I was not so fond of playing that kind of music, I had spent most of my life with a guitar on my lap. I had spent most of my life dreaming of a career in country music.

She saw the look on my face, and put her hand up before her eyes. "Oh!" She whispered. "Oh... I'm sorry... I shouldn't ask that of you. I'm sorry."

I paid the check, left a small tip and we went outside and drove home, saying very little as we drove. When we got to the house, she rushed inside and went straight away to the bedroom, and was already in bed when I finished in the bathroom and went in. I got into bed, put my arm around her and pulled her to me and whispered. "I hate square-dance music, anyhow."

CHAPTER TWENTY TWO

Memories are both wonderful and awesome. It's amazing how the mind can bring back memories so fresh, so real. It's almost inconceivable that one can travel back to the distant past and see, smell, and feel as if no time had passed. How memories can swim the ocean and climb snow covered mountains. How the memory of an angel tiptoeing through the surf at Mexico beach can bring tears to an old man's eyes.

As I sit here beside her grave, my mind rushes back to the time she sat with me at the Partridge in Rome and ask me not to work at the square dance any more. I can see the blush in her eyes as she looked across the table and almost whispered those words. And I am glad that I answered, "I hate square-dance music, anyhow."

I remember that the next week was a busy time for us. I found a new job, and we rented our first house. The job came about when I met John Davis at the Home Store. John lived near my parents in the Bellah subdivision.

"Hi Curley!" he said. "I heard you were back in town. How are things going?"

"Just fine," I ventured.

"Heard you got married… working anyplace?"

"I've been working down at the Hanger, you know, the square-dance. Just quit though… I'm sorter looking for a job now."

"Well, that's great. I'm sorter looking for somebody like you to fill a job. Me 'n Mose… that's my law partner… well we recently bought into the Hall-Craft boat company down in Lyerly. You know Herman Hall?"

"Don't think so." I said.

"Well, Herman's a great fellow, and if you think you'd like to build boats, go down and tell him I sent you. I believe you'll like that… I know you've been helping Mr. Ponder in the building trade. I don't think building boats is much different from building houses." He laughed and patted me on the back. "Glad to see you back."

I drove down to Lyerly that very afternoon, and John was right… I did like Herman Hall, and I was sure I was going to like working at the little Hall-Craft boat factory.

Getting into our new rented house was a little harder. We spent almost three days looking at furniture that we could not afford, and finally opened an account at Sears and bought enough to furnish the three room duplex sparingly. And when the furniture finally came, we spent the weekend setting it up and hanging curtains, etc.

It is needless to say that the remainder of 1948 was the happiest time of my life. Bunton, I soon learned, was a meticulous house keeper. She had learned much from her grandmother... Mamaw. Mamaw was the only mother she had ever known, since her mother had died when she was only three years old. And due to Mamaw's training, our little house became the neatest house in town.

In the mornings, Herman Hall would pick me up for the seven mile ride to Lyerly and bring me back in the evenings, and Bunton would meet me at the door bubbling over with joy that I was home.

During the week, usually on Tuesdays and Thursdays, I would go to the airport and fly that old J-3 cub for a couple of hours and then drive back to Summerville and pick Bunton up for a little drive before supper.

And then, on her 18th birthday June 13, 1948 I gave her the birthday present I had made for her at the boat shop. When I brought the little laminated Maplewood dressing table in and sat it down in the bedroom, her eyes lit up like a couple of candles. She rushed into my arms, and we stood for a long time holding each other very close. And then, we walked back into the living room and sat down on the sofa.

"I love the dressing table," she said. "Now I have something to tell you."

My heart pounded a little faster. I feared, due to the serious look on her face, that she was about to give me bad news. And then she smiled and placed her hand on her abdomen.

"Guess what?" She whispered.

Well, that 'what' turned out to be that beautiful little girl we call Claudette.

When we told my family about the upcoming event, Daddy thought it over for a moment and said. "You gonna start that kind of foolishness, I guess we better build you a better place to live."

Of course, I'm sure that he had been thinking about that for some time now. I had noticed him measuring, and stepping off space in the lower part of his yard several times. And I had been right.

"Come on out here," he motioned to me one afternoon. We walked out in the yard and he handed me the end of a steel measuring tape.

"Hold this and stand right here," he said, pointing to a small tuft of grass. Then he walked towards the back of the yard and laid a small rock on the ground. He motioned and I carried the end of the tape to where he stood, and he walked a distance towards the lower side of the lot and placed another rock on the ground. After the two remaining sides of a square were marked, Daddy stood back with a pleasant expression on his slightly wrinkled face, and said,

"Looks just right for three rooms and a bath. What you think?"

"Well actually," I said. "I think we have a little bit of a problem."

"How's that?"

"Last time I checked," I grinned, "fellow needs a little cash to build a house." Daddy started to walk back towards the house.

"I think we might be able to work something out 'bout that."

So, within a week, we were digging trenches for the foundation of our first house.

CHAPTER TWENTY THREE

During the remainder of that year, Daddy and I worked on the little house as often as we could, and it seemed sometimes that things were going mighty slow. However, we both had full time jobs to run. I worked eight hours a day five days a week, and sometimes another four hours on Saturdays, and Daddy was in the process of building a barn and some other out buildings for what we called a 'city slicker', who had recently bought a farm in the county.

Due to working on the house in my spare time, I had to give up flying and a few other things temporarily. And, of course Bunton and I were not able to take so many long drives as we had been doing earlier. But, seeing the house go up, and watching Bunton blossom into the most beautiful woman-with-child in the world, was more than compensation for missing out on flying that old J3 Cub and all the other stuff.

Later in the year when the house was almost done, due to Momma's insistence we moved back into the house with her and Daddy until the baby was born. And then on January 19th, Claudette... you know, the one who plays the piano almost better than Van Cliburn, came to live with us.

On or around April first 1949, we moved into our new little house on South Edmondson Street, and I decided that I should try to get a little better education in order to raise a family. So consequently, I quit my job at the boat factory, took a nightshift job at the cotton mill, and started to school at North Georgia Business College in Rome.

I really wanted to study law but could not find a law school close enough to Summerville that would accept me. And, the GI bill of rights would not only pay for my tuition and books at North Georgia Business College, but actually paid GI students $120.00 monthly subsistence allowance. Now, that might not sound like very much in today's world, but in 1949, that was almost as much as I made a month for working forty hours per week in the cotton mill.

One Saturday evening, shortly after we moved into the new house, Bunton came into the living room where I was sitting, and asked. "Would you mind if we go to the Baptist church this week?"

"Why not?" I said. "After all the bugger man's gonna get us all in the end."

"Why do you say that," she almost whispered. "I hope you don't really think that. If you do... if you really believe that, I think you really need to pray for forgiveness. The Bible says that *'If you have faith like a grain of mustard seed, you will say to this mountain, move from here to there, and it will move'.* Don't you believe that?"

"Well," I said. "I will be glad to go with you to the Baptist church, but don't hand me no shovel... I don't think I'm quite ready to move Lookout Mountain yet."

The next morning when we told Momma and Daddy that we were going to the Baptist church, Momma looked at Daddy with obvious disappointment. I felt sure that Bunton noticed the expression on Momma's face but I knew that neither of them would mention it.

When we got in the car and started I thought we were going to the Pennville Gospel Tabernacle. "I thought you belonged to a nondenominational church," I said.

"I do," she smiled. "But today, we're going to South Summerville." And when we got to the church, I was surprised. Everybody knew Bunton, and everybody seemed very pleased that we had come.

When church started, I had another surprise coming. After the choir finished, and was seated in the congregation, the preacher got up and said.

"Turn to Matthew 25:41-46" and started to read. *'Then he will say to those on his left, 'Depart from me, you cursed, into the eternal fire prepared for the devil and his angels. And these will go away into eternal punishment, but the righteous into eternal life.'*

"Now turn to Romans 2:6" *'He will render to each one according to his works: to those who by patience in well-doing seek for glory and honor and immortality, he will give eternal life; but for those who are self-seeking and do not obey the truth, but obey unrighteousness, there will be wrath and fury.'*

"Now turn to Revelation 21:8" *'But as for the cowardly, the faithless, the detestable, as for murderers, the sexually immoral, sorcerers, idolaters, and all liars, their portion will be in the lake that burns with fire and sulfur, which is the second death.'*

I didn't listen to most of the rest of the sermon. These people were teaching the same line that I had heard all my life.

CHAPTER TWENTY FOUR

I didn't mention what I had been thinking at church to Bunton. I had learned that she was very faithful to her Christian beliefs, and I knew that she would worry about me, if I told her how I really felt. She had been quite devoted to going to church, even if we had been attending the Church of God. And I had noticed that she had not shown any resentment when remarks were made by the preacher, or our Sunday school teacher that all but slandered people of other faiths.

In any event, aside from the problem I had with doubt, our lives were going quite well. She would always get up quite early in order to cook a good breakfast in time for me to eat leisurely before starting down the road to Rome. In the afternoons, I had arranged to cut the last class in order to get home in time to have a few moments with Bunton and the baby before going to the cotton mill. And then, on Saturday mornings, I would go back to Rome and make up the classes missed during the week. On Saturday evenings and Sundays, we made up for all the time spent apart. We would visit nearby parks or drive someplace like Lookout Mountain and have a picnic on the brink of the highest cliff. Sometimes, we would go to a movie in Rome, and have dinner at one of the many fine restaurants... when we could manage to have enough money left.

And then, on Monday, June 13th 1949, I left school at noon in order to get home in time to present her with the little necklace I had bought for her birthday. When I entered the front door, she came out of the kitchen where she had been cleaning the stove and rushed into the bathroom to wash her face and comb her hair.

"What are you doing home?" She stammered, when she came back into the living room. "You're supposed to let me know," She came over to the couch where I sat and snuggled up beside me. "Well?" She asked shyly.

"Thought I'd come home in time to give you this," I ventured, as I removed the little necklace from my pocket, and placed it around her neck.

She ran to the bedroom to view the little gold plated necklace in the mirror, and said as she returned, "I knew you would get this for me. That's the reason I spent so much time looking at it last week at Jackson's." Then she sat back down on the couch beside me.

"Got another little surprise for you," she smiled as she placed her hand on her tummy the same way she did on her 18th birthday the year before.

That little surprise turned out to be our other pretty little gal Jenette, you know... the Master of Language-arts teacher who cannot teach her father... the jackleg, un-sung novelist, the faults of colloquialism. She came to live with us on January 13th 1950, just six days before Claudette's first birthday.

CHAPTER TWENTY FIVE

Today is the first day of 2013, and as Ooda and I sit here at her grave, memories of Bunton, and of our almost sixty-five years together flow back into my mind like an avalanche.

Speaking of Ooda, he's my little dog. He was named after Saddam Hussein's unruly son. But, Ooda is everything but unruly. He has been my constant companion ever since Bunton died. He sleeps beside my bed at night, and goes everywhere I go during the day. He sits with me at Bunton's grave and appears to almost cry when I cry. However, I am sure that Ooda doesn't feel all the pain that I feel... I am sure that he doesn't cry in his sleep because of some hurt he has caused her. Ooda only knew her for a very short time... and though I'm sure that he learned to love her as almost everybody who knew her did, he has never spoken a harsh word to her. He has only snuggled up to her, and enjoyed the warmth of her presence, a wonderful memory that we have in common.

Sitting here with her on New Year's Day shadows the sorrow with a bit of pleasure, as I look at the beautiful Christmas flowers we placed on her grave... and a rush of thankfulness when I remember the words Jimmy Bryant spoke at her funeral.

And then on October 26th he wrote:

"My dear grieving friend,

While the funeral services for Mrs. Frances provided me the opportunity to speak some formal words in her memory, I also want to share a private thought or two. In addition, I want to take this opportunity to express my deep appreciation to you for the honor of participating in the memorial service for one of my most ardent encouragers.

Now that the service is over, and family and friends have returned to their own homes and responsibilities, I can imagine that you are feeling Mrs. Frances' absence more than ever. The wisdom of those who have lived through a similar loss is that time eventually brings healing for grief. Although that may sound impossible in the midst of your present sorrow, I pray that comfort will come to you quickly. The Lord will not leave you nor forsake you. Hold fast to these words of Jesus; 'Peace I leave with you; my peace I give to you.' I realize that I am writing to one that has a certain peace already. The love you all had for Mrs. Frances, the kind loving care you gave her, and the best of provisions that you made for her gives you a sense of peace because in your heart you know that you did everything a husband and a family can do for a loved one. It is so encouraging to see the love that your extended family has for you as well. It is a rare and uplifting experience to see such love expressed so sincerely.

I am sure that there will be good days and some days that are not so good. You will surely miss her, some days more than others. However, the joy of knowing that she is in glory with her Savior and others whom she loved that went on before will make those 'not so good days' more bearable.

In addition, Ester and I want to thank you for the more than generous gift. It was certainly not expected or anticipated. However, we do appreciate it. More than the gift however, we appreciate your friendship. We thank God for each of you and cherish you among our dearest friends.

If we can ever help in any way, do not hesitate to let us know. We love you all.

Your friends and His servants,

Jimmy and Esther"

Many others have spoken words of condolence and encouragement, and each has been greatly appreciated. One never knows how to cherish such kindness until he or she is on the receiving end. However, when the lights are out, the sound of kind words vanishes, to be replaced with the flow of memories that reach far back into the past.

Today, I am carried back to the summer of 1952. In March of that year our third little girl was born. However, unfortunately she passed away the same day, without either of us having the thrill of holding her in our arms. We named her Melissa Margret, mainly because Margret rhymed with Claudette, and Jenette.

Today, I am saddened that little Melissa Margret never had the chance to know her mother, Mary Frances (Bunton) Ponder. Never actually had that chance, until now.

CHAPTER TWENTY SIX

Near the end of June of 1952, I finished my education at North Georgia Business College where I completed graduate courses in Higher Accounting and Business Administration, as well as Tax Law and Accounting, and other related subjects. Also I was in the midst of studies in Commercial Law … training that would be invaluable in my life's career.

I had opened a small office in downtown Summerville, and being the optimist that I am, had started to remodel our little house on South Edmonson Street.

When we had finished the remodeling, sometime in October, our friends Leonard and Betty Parker came to visit us. The Parkers had two children about the same age as ours, and we enjoyed their visit immensely. We took them and the kids up to Lake Winnipesauke near Chattanooga, and out to Desoto Falls on Lookout Mountain. As we were sitting at the water falls, and I admitted that my business was not taking off too swiftly, Leonard suggested that we move down to Columbus. He was sure that I could find a good paying job in a city that size. As a matter of fact, he knew about an opening at a finance company in Phoenix City just across the bridge from Columbus.

Consequently, after much consideration, we decided to take him up and arranged to go down and live with them for a couple of weeks and look things over.

It turned out that the Bell Finance Company was happy to have a graduate of North Georgia Business College and signed me up right away as their credit manager, a good sounding title that turned out to be nothing but a bill collector.

As a matter of fact, Bell Finance Company was the kind of organization usually referred to as "loan shark". I was totally unprepared for the kind of things I was getting myself into.

As you probably already know, in 1952 Phoenix City Alabama was well known as the "Crime city of the south." I refer you to the book, "The Tragedy and the Triumph of Phoenix City, Alabama" by Margaret Anne Barnes. As an aspiring novelist myself looking for a publisher, I was fortunate to meet with Ms. Barnes when she was doing the research for that book, and was able to give her a little information which she said was helpful to her cause.

To make a long story short, I learned quite soon all I needed to know about "Sin City South"... things that I couldn't tell Bunton for fear that she would be ready to move back to Summerville before the telling was through.

Several weeks later, after facing a number of punks with knives, and having a shotgun, a pistol, and a butcher knife pulled on me, I quit the big "Credit Manager" job and took a position at the Columbus Detective Agency. My first case there was a domestic surveillance case. After collecting sufficient evidence to support the client in divorce litigation, I learned that the man the client's wife was seeing was one of Phoenix City's most notorious racketeers.

Consequently, shortly thereafter, Bunton and I moved back to Summerville, Georgia.

Through all of this trauma... the trauma of moving to a strange city, of sitting alone with two little girls in a shabby, rented apartment, of moving back home to find our pretty little house severely damaged by renters who had not even paid the rent they owed us... Bunton was calm and supportive of my bumbling efforts to find and build a better existence for our family. And through it all, we found happiness in the reality of being together.

Back in Summerville, after we had replaced a few window panes, fixed a few holes in the sheetrock walls, and painted the house inside and out, we settled down and determined to make our little house a real home... a home that our children could remember with affection. I rented office space on North Commerce Street and started in earnest to build an accounting practice that would survive until this day.

To augment my income until the practice was large enough to support us, I took a job in the lab at Regal Textile

Corporation, at Trion, Georgia, about five miles up Highway 27 from Summerville.

A few weeks after we were back in church at the Church of God on Bellah Avenue, Bunton found the girls crying when she picked them up at the church nursery after service. It seems that the nursery attendant had been teaching the little tikes about God and the Devil.

Although they were very young, they could understand much of what they were being taught, especially Claudette and some of the other older children.

"Mommy, Mommy," Claudette cried. "Mommy! Bugger man… Bugger man makes fire. Mommy, fire burns… fire burns." She knew about fire, and that fire burns because we had tried to teach them to stay away from fire, to stay away from the stove when Mommy was cooking, and to never play with matches, etc.

CHAPTER TWENTY SEVEN

Bunton didn't tell me about the incident at church until later the next Saturday evening. The girls were visiting next door with Momma and Daddy. When I finished trimming the grass around the flower beds out back and came into the house, she followed me into the living room and sat down across the room from the couch where I sat.

"Would you mind if we start going to South Summerville?" she asked. I knew that she was referring to the South Summerville Baptist church.

"Why not?" I answered. "We're all going to the same purgatory anyhow."

"I wish you wouldn't say things like that." She looked at me with obvious hurt showing on her face. I reached out my hand and she came over and sat down on the couch.

"Well," she almost whispered. "Something happened at church last Sunday. I don't want to take the girls there anymore." I sat up straight, and looked at her, and she turned her head and looked down at the floor. Then when she looked like she was about to cry, I pulled her to me and sat quietly, waiting for her to continue.

She told me about the incident that caused the girls to cry, and I agreed with her whole-heartedly. She had been totally agreeable about where we had been going to church ever since our marriage and I had not given the matter any thought. To me, it seemed logical that a wife would attend the church of a husband's choice. But now that I thought of it, I felt a pang of guilt because I had not discussed the matter with her before.

"Don't worry," I whispered. "We'll go to church anywhere you want to."

"What will your mother and daddy think?" She asked. "I know they don't approve of the Baptist faith. You think they'll be mad at us?"

"No! I don't think they'll be mad... a little disappointed maybe, but not mad."

Well, I was right about them being 'disappointed'. When I talked to them later that evening, Momma almost cried.

"Now you know what's right," she said. "You know that some of those people think that it's alright to sin a little every day, so long as they go to church on Sunday." Daddy cleared his throat.

"Now, Emmie! Bunton's been real good 'bout going to church with us. She has her own faith, and she has the right to go to her church if she wants to. We can't tell her what to do. We can only set a good example, and hope she makes the right decision. Anyhow, some of them Baptists are good folks... you know that."

I decided that it was best not to tell them about the reason we were changing. We started going to South Summerville that week and about three weeks later, Bunton went to the altar and asked that her letter of membership be moved from the Pennville Gospel Tabernacle to the South Summerville Baptist Church. She made no attempt to persuade me to join and seemed grateful that I did not object to her joining.

Later that year we attended several nights of a gospel revival at the Church of God and continued to attend South Summerville on Sundays. When Claudette and Jenette were old enough to attend Sunday school, Bunton carried them into their first class and sat with them. And, from that day forward, the Baptist faith had two additional, totally devoted members.

It's hard to go back and relate to all the wonderful things that were happening to us at that time. I passed the examination and became a member of the National Society of Public accountants... I was the only practicing accountant in Chattooga County, Georgia at that time, and my practice was growing with leaps and bounds.

Bunton, in addition to the wonderful time she was having buying the most beautiful clothes she could find for herself and the girls, was busy helping in the nursery at church on Sundays, working to help her aunt Beth with the housekeeping at the Gilmer house, and bowling one evening a week with a group of friends.

At the same time I decided that even if the GI bill would no longer pay for my flying lessons, I could afford to continue on my own. Consequently, I went down to the Rome air field and made arrangements to fly with Mr. Barry Woods, one of North Georgia's best known flight instructors.

Over the next two or three years, almost everything I touched seemed to turn to money. The accounting phase of my practice grew to a point where I was required to hire two fulltime assistants to do the daily write-ups, and the tax service portion was drawing clients from as far away as Atlanta and Chattanooga.

In the meantime, I resigned from my job in the lab at Regal Textile Corporation, where I had been working half-asleep on the night shift, allowing a little more time for us to enjoy this wonderful new life together with our two beautiful little girls and a host of friends.

And, from what I have said before, you probably have already guessed that we were draining our new-found fountain of wealth almost faster than receiving it.

CHAPTER TWEITY EIGHT

At the end of the tax season in the spring of 1956, we decided to do additional remodeling to our house on South Edmonson Street.

One morning when Uncle Fred and I were up on the roof working, Bunton called me to the phone. When I spoke the traditional 'Hello' into the mouthpiece, I was inundated with a flood of chatter with a slight Yankee accent, which I recognized as my old war time buddy, Mario Sisconi. Of course, Sisconi was not his real name. I use that name here as I did in my previous writing for the same reasons.

Mario and I had parted company on unfriendly terms when I left New York City early in 1947... And we had not corresponded with each other since. It's needless to say that I was surprised to hear from him after all this time, especially after the things that had been said when we parted.

"Hey, Reb!" He chanted. "Get the little woman and kids in the car and point that thing down to Fort Lauderdale."

I remembered that Mario's family owned a motel in Fort Lauderdale.

"Afraid I can't make it, Dago," I answered. "How'd you know I have a wife and kids? You been spying on me, man?"

"Hey, Reb! You left the family... family didn't leave you. After all, you might guess that we'd want to keep up with you. Surely you don't think Daddy would not ask about you from time to time. Come on now... tote it on down to Lauderdale. Me 'n yous need to bury the old hatchet man. Come on now, let's have a little fun and catch up on stuff."

I knew that there was no use for me to ask Bunton to go. I had already told her too much about Mario and the business his family was in. As a matter of fact, Mario's family name had been in the national news on at least one occasion that Bunton knew about.

"I'm sorry, Dago," I said. "I've got too many things going right now. I appreciate the invitation, but I just can't go right now. Maybe we can do something later on?"

"OK, Reb! It was just a thought. I thought about you when we came to this little town in South Carolina. Ever been to Summerville, South Carolina Reb?"

"No... don't think so?" I said.

"OK, Reb. Write this down," he spat.

I found pencil and paper, and said. "OK, Dago," and Mario gave me the name, location and phone number of the Sisconi family motel in Fort Lauderdale.

"Take the girls down there any time you want to. Call ahead and accommodations will be arranged. We have a restaurant on the premises, so all you need to bring is your toothbrush and clothes. I'll tell them when we get down there," he continued. "You don't need money, boy... you know that. After all, I still owe yous a couple of bucks."

We said goodbye and hung up, and that was the last time I was ever to hear from my old friend, Mario Sisconi. He checked out on the streets of Yonkers, New York sometime in 1966, as his wife Mary would tell me many years later.

One morning while I was at the office, Bunton called and asked me to come home. My mother had become suddenly ill. It turned out that she suffered the sudden rupture of an un-known cerebral aneurysm. She passed away within forty-eight hours after admission to the little Summerville hospital.

Consequently, grief-stricken and in need of a break from our active lifestyle, we decided to take a vacation... the first one we had ever shared.

And, having recently had memories of the beautiful white-sand beaches of Florida brought to mind, I suggested that we go to Panama City for a few days. I knew that it would be useless to suggest accepting Mario's invitation for the free use of rooms and services at the Sisconi family motel in Fort Lauderdale.

CHAPTER TWENTY NINE

Getting ready to go on vacation turned out to be just about as much fun as going. Bunton spent days shopping for pretty little sun-dresses, big bouncy balloon balls, sand-buckets and shovels, and bathing suits for all, and I was busy locating a big truck size inner-tube, folding lounge chairs, and wondering if our money would run out before we even got started.

I wanted to go in the sporty little Buick hardtop we had recently acquired. I felt like a millionaire tooling around town in that pretty little red and white machine, especially when pulling our new red and white 14 foot runabout in which I had added white leatherette upholstery to match the car. But, there was no way to get all the luggage, toys, boxes and pretty little girls in that contraption. So, consequently, we set in one evening to load our paraphernalia into the Plymouth.

When the clock alarmed the next morning, two pretty little girls, and two tired, sleepy eyed parents jumped out of bed and headed South down U.S. Highway 27.

Bunton was a radiant beauty that morning, sitting back in her seat with the window half-down, and long strands of silky auburn hair hanging over the back of the seat. The girls were having a ball counting cows and horses and comparing the number of black cars to that of white, or blue, or red. At Columbus, I wanted to drive by Baker Village and show the girls where we had lived for a while when they were mere babies. However with slightly more than half the estimated daylight driving time ahead of us, we decided to just stop for a quick lunch and continue driving. We even decided against calling Leonard and Betty to meet us for lunch. That, we knew would take up more time than visiting Baker Village.

When we were back in the car... across the 14th Street bridge and headed South down U. S. Highway 431, Bunton led the choir in a number of songs the girls liked to sing. "Jesus loves me! This I know, for the Bible tells me so. Little ones to Him belong; they are weak, but He is strong."

Finally, when four or five songs had been sung four or five times, she took out the little Bible she always seemed to have handy, and started to read.

"Children, obey your parents in the Lord, for this is right. "Honor your father and mother" (this is the first commandment with a promise), "that it may go well with you and that you may live long in the land." Fathers, do not provoke your children to anger, but bring them up in the discipline and instruction of the Lord."

"Mommy, what's comman'er mean?"

"That means that Jesus said 'be good... do what Mommy and Daddy tells you to do and Jesus will be glad."

"What's 'be glad?'"

"Come on now! You know what be glad means."

Gradually the banter subsided and the only sound to invade my subconscious reverie was the sound of tires on pavement, and the pleasant hiss of wind coming through slightly cracked windows. Bunton kneeled and reached over the back of her seat to cover the girls with a blanket and then sat back and closed her eyes.

I looked at her and marveled at the faith she exhibited in her belief in God, and the gentle way she was teaching the girls the meaning of the scripture much in the same way my parents had taught me.

"Mommy, what's comman'er mean?"

Yes indeed! I thought. Why could I not fully believe the wonderful notion that a real God exists? A God that created the Heaven and earth, and provided a way for my own salvation... a way for me to exist perpetually, without guilt or condemnation. "Mommy, what's comman'er mean?"... Indeed:

It means, though shalt not! I thought. But, what if?

"Well, I guess," the preacher had said. "I guess, a fellow has to do what he has to do."

Why could I not fully believe that? Why could I not even discuss it with Bunton? She seemed to understand more about the Bible than I, even considering the fact that her family was not so deeply steeped in the Christian faith, as was mine. Why could I not fully believe when I had had so many things happened to me that should have convinced me. What about the strange manner in which both my parents, and the lady Burgomaster of the little French village had been forewarned that their children (me and the pretty girl Monique) were about to crash into the old rock house? How somehow, they knew in advance that our lives were in danger?

Finally, I came back to the present, looked at the gas meter, and noticed that the hand was brushing the big E. When I pulled over for gas, Bunton opened her eyes and said... "Where are we?"

"I think we're just about there," I ventured. "Sign some time back said 22 miles."

An old man wearing a straw hat came out and started to fill our tank, and when he noticed all the luggage, and stuff in the car, he asked.

"Going to the beach?"

"Yes! How far," I asked.

"Bout ten miles... you got reservation?"

"No. Didn't think it would be necessary this late in the year."

The old man took my money and made change and swiped at the windshield with a dirty rag.

"Boy… you should have got reservation. School kids out. Boy… they got that place covered like a snow storm. People are sleeping on the beach. Boy… you should have got reservation."

I thanked him and pulled out into the highway, and the first thing I saw was a motel sign showing the flashing word, VACANCY. I pulled over and talked to Bunton about what the old man had said, and we decided it best to take a room there in that grungy-looking old log-cabin motel that looked like Aunt Jemima's country home.

So we pulled in, gave our ten dollar bill to another old man who looked very much like the one at the service station, and spent one of the most miserable nights of our lives with a large family of over-sized cockroaches.

CHAPTER THIRTY

It's January 8th, and she has been lying here under this cold mound of dirt for three whole months. During that eternity, I have missed visiting her only one day... a day when I was deathly sick. On each of the other days, I have visited perhaps an average of three times... and like today, have sat with a wash of memories that are sometimes impossible to describe. Admittedly, I strive to recall only the pleasant ones... a task that is not usually easy to achieve. In fact, there are many that bring a flood of tears... tears of regret, because as human beings, our lives together have sometimes been mired with disagreement, disappointment, and hurt... and it's needless to say that I have shed a river of tears over every hurtful thing I ever did to her.

I have often heard people say that through a long life of marriage they have never had a disagreement... never spoken unkindly, or done anything to hurt each other. If you are one of those, I wish to invite you to breakfast some morning at the liars table at Jim's Family Restaurant, in Summerville, Georgia. In case I am not there when you arrive, I will tell Sewell, Ralph and Doug to extend to you a cordial welcome. As a matter of fact, I will ask that you be seated next to Bob at the head of the table. I am sure you will be a welcome asset to our little group, even if your membership should cause some, such as Jim and Jerry concern regarding there ranking.

If you really never did anything that you regret... something that could harm your marital relationship, something that you wish had never happened... then you my friend are one of the rarest creatures known to man.

Unfortunately, I cannot honestly claim that I have never caused hurt to invade the otherwise wonderful journey through life Bunton and I have enjoyed together. Consequently, it is with an immense measure of relief that I am now able to return to the wonderful memories of our first vacation together.

After the miserable night we spent at the Cockroach Inn, just north of Panama City, we drove on into town and as we drove across the Hathaway bridge and entered the beach area, almost every motel along the miles-long stretch of Long Beach displayed a vacancy sign. It was obvious that we had been duped by the old man at the service station the evening before.

However, we quickly put this aside as the girls chattered and danced with joy at their first ever look at the Gulf of Mexico.

"Mommy, Mommy... look!" they shouted. "Look Mommy, look at the water. It's so big, Mommy... It's so big."

Because we now had all day to select a place to stay, we had a leisurely breakfast at a small beach-side restaurant, and decided to drive east along the coast before making a decision.

After a few miles of beautiful, white-sand beaches, we came to the then small community of Mexico Beach. At that time, Mexico Beach consisted of a small number of private houses and a few places of business, including a grocery store and restaurant on the north side of highway 98, and three almost new motels on the beach side.

We decided that this was exactly what we were looking for. We wanted a lot of uncluttered beach, with a world of privacy... and that was exactly what Mexico Beach turned out to be.

Today as I look back at that time in memory, I am overcome with emotion... and awash with joy as I watch Bunton and the girls gleefully racing up and down the beach. I can see her asleep on a large beach towel, and wading in the surf with a pretty little girl holding each hand. I watch her in nostalgic longing as I recall the beauty of her sitting on the balcony feeding sea gulls with popcorn. And I yearn for the smoothness of her embrace.

CHAPTER THIRTY ONE

Over the next several years we became a regular fixture at Panama City Beach. As a matter of fact, the personnel at the Casa Loma motel came to know us by first names and welcomed the four of us at least one time and sometimes twice each year. And then we discovered Long Boat Key and started to explore the Gulf shores from Tampa Bay to Anna Maria Island, Bradenton, and south to Naples.

At the risk of getting the cart before the horse, later on one of our wealthy clients gave us a week-long vacation each year for several years. During that time, we explored the east coast from Jekyll Island Georgia south to West Palm Beach.

Back home we discovered water skiing and spent at least a half-day each week someplace on a river or lake. We started at the little lake at Cloudland, Georgia and graduated to the Tennessee River at Scottsboro, Alabama, and then we went north to Harrison's Bay near Chattanooga, and south to a little lake known as Sea-Breeze. Sometimes we would overnight on the lake at Altoona... and then the big lake Weise was finished near our home, and we settled in for a years-long love affair with that beautiful body of water. Although Bunton never learned to swim, she became one of the best skiers on the water.

Sitting here at her grave as I said before, I try to recall only memories of the good times we had together, and watching her on water skis was certainly one of the good ones. "Look Daddy, Mommy can fly. Let me Daddy, let me do that"... and I can almost hear Claudette and Jenette scream at the sight of their mother sailing across the water. Before long, they too could soar across the waves, like a bird.

During that time life was a wonderful dream-filled journey, etching a kaleidoscope of memories on my mind that would last a lifetime. And, although I did not fully appreciate the fortunes God had given me, in retrospect I can now see that the luckiest day of my life was the day I first met Bunton at that little grocery store on Commerce Street in Summerville... the day I gave her a lemon as a birthday gift... something she would tease me about on many occasions throughout life.

First of all, she unknowingly helped to erase memories that had robbed me of countless night's sleep... and eased worries that my soul was destined to an eternity of hell-fire and brimstone.

As a matter of fact, I had begun to purge from mind, doubts that there really was a God, and that he was merciful towards ungrateful sorts such as I. However, due to my insistence that we go to the river, or lake at least once each week, we were not going to church regularly. Nonetheless,

Bunton insisted that the girls be carried to Sunday school each Sunday morning before we left for such an outing.

Otherwise, life seemed almost perfect. For the first time in both our lives, we had money to buy the things we needed, and almost enough to satisfy all the things we wanted. My practice was growing rapidly, especially the tax service side. And, although the tax code was not nearly as complicated then as now, it was obvious that the long months and years I had dedicated to the study of tax law was paying off. By then, and virtually because of word-of-mouth advertising, tax clients were coming from as far away as Atlanta, Chattanooga, Birmingham, and even Baton Rouge Louisiana.

In the spring of 1959, almost without any consultation with Bunton, and certainly without her wholehearted approval, I started the process of building a new house. Earlier, I had become friends with a young man whose grandfather was principal founder of a savings and loan association in Rome. And through my often visits there, the VP at that institution felt secure in telling me that they would lend me all the money I might need when the house was finished. However, after he and the founder came to inspect the house, he called me next day and said that the value was certainly there, but because the house was in Summerville, they would have to limit the amount of the loan. Consequently, what they offered came to several thousand dollars less than the amount I needed, making it necessary for me to borrow from our local bank to make up the difference.

Bunton had tried to tell me that we were spending far too much money, but I was adamant that I could always make more by simply working a little harder. And, due to hard work and good luck, the bank loan was soon behind us. However, I was not broke from the habit of spending, and Bunton was unable to convince me that we should be saving for the future... on the other hand, I must admit that she was still fond of pretty dresses and things, both for herself and the girls.

To add to our problems, it was necessary for us to buy almost a full house of new furniture, and one of the cars decided to take a rest... and of course, Bunton would like to have a nicer car than the old Buick she had been driving. After all, she reasoned, now that the girls were cheerleaders and engaged in so many affairs at school, we should not want to see them carted around in a rattletrap.

Well... she didn't have to tease me like that. I was ready to step up to a big old Wildcat Buick.

And now that I think of it, it's hard to see how we survived over the next fifteen, or sixteen years.

CHAPTER THIRTY TWO

At some point in time during that period... we, at Bunton's insistence, started back to church. South Summerville had a new pastor, the Reverend Smith... and he and I developed a good rapport from the very start. After a few friendly visits to my home and office, one might have thought that we were a couple of redneck mud-racers to hear us kid each other. Upon our arrival at church, "Preach," as I called him, would say something like... "Did he wash behind his ears, Bunton?" And I would ask him not to preach so loud... "I need a little nap," I'd say.

Well that might sound like a lot of foolishness... but if you really are a redneck mud-racer you might understand that things are about to get serious when we all get inside the church.

Preach could really put you to thinking about all those things my mother had tried to teach me in my youth. And, after listing to him for a bunch of Sundays, I went up to the altar and made my confession the way the Baptists teach. Everybody at church that morning seemed happy that I was joining their ranks, and a date for a baptismal service was set.

There was no doubt that Bunton was pleased with the decision I had made. I knew that she had prayed for me much longer and harder than had the Reverend Smith. The girls seemed overjoyed that Daddy was finally acting like a daddy should, and I am sure that my mother... had she still been living, would have been pleased, even if I had joined a Baptist church.

However, a couple of Sundays after the baptismal rites were performed, Reverend Smith announced that he was resigning as pastor at South Summerville. The reason he gave was as follows.

"I've been praying for Henderson Ponder ever since we first met... and when he walked down the aisle and gave his heart to the Lord a couple of weeks ago, I knew that my mission at the South Summerville Baptist church was over."

That really made me feel bad. As a matter of fact, I had not completely divorced myself of the doubts that had caused me to lie awake a thousand nights and worry. The Bible plainly says *"Thou shalt not!"* However, even the preacher at the Bellah Avenue Church of God had not seemed to be sure that some of the *"Thou shalt not's"* were absolute. But my thinking was, if the commandment, *"Thou shat not kill"* is a true commandment of God, why then are the scriptures filled with examples of God, urging tribal leaders to wage war.

Example: Deuteronomy 20:4 *For the Lord your God is he that goes with you, to fight for you against your enemies, to save you.*

Example: 1 Chronicles 5:20: *And they were helped against them, and the Hagarites were delivered into their hand, and all that were with them: for they cried to God in the battle, and he was entreated of them; because they put their trust in him.*

Example: Matthew 10:34 *"Do not think that I have come to bring peace to the earth. I have not come to bring peace, but a sword."*

The Church of God preacher at Berryton had said that if you did not obey Gods commandments, you were bound to suffer throughout eternity in the 'Lake of fire. And then, that fellow at the Bellah Avenue Church had proclaimed, "I guess, a fellow has to do what he has to do."

In any event, that was a time I really tried to shape up and live the kind of life my parents, and the girl I married wanted me to live. However, the new pastor that came to South Summerville after Reverend Smith left was less than friendly with me and my family. He seemed to latch on to a certain little clique of members and paid little attention to the rest. I suppose that I should have invited him to a chicken dinner... but, all kidding aside, one would think that a minister would at least be friendly with a new convert. However, to tell the truth the man was, in my opinion, a poor excuse for a preacher in the first place. Consequently I drifted off into the same lackadaisical attitude I had espoused for so long.

Also, there were other distractions to wrest my mind from the perplexities I had encountered in my quest to understand the church and its teachings. And without telegraphing my disenchantment to Bunton as much as possible, I mentally drifted away from the church and sought other fulfillments in what the preacher would call secular things.

The first of those "secular procurements", and as usual without consultation with Bunton, was the purchase of our first cruiser-type sailboat. This is something I had wanted since I was a little tyke racing up and down the banks of Raccoon Creek. And to me it was indeed a beautiful thing... a twenty-five foot Davis craft all wood boat named "The Leaky Teki"... which, at that time, stood out like a sore thumb in the waters of Lake Weiss.

Just as I had expected, Bunton showed little interest in my latest venture. And now, after all these years, I must admit that she was right in what she said when my little poor-boy's yacht found a resting place on the bottom of Lake Weise during a storm, "A sail boat is a great way to pour money into the lake".

CHAPTER THIRTY THREE

When the girls finished their college education, got married and moved off to South Carolina and Indiana respectively, it seemed that Bunton lost interest in the house, the one we called our "Big House" on Peach Orchard Hill. At that time, I closed my branch office in La Fayette... the last of my failed adventures in chain operations, and again without much consultation with her, sold the house and built another (the house where I now live) on the three-acre wooded plot of land just down the hill from our old house. I had admired that property for many years.

Near the same time, I moved my office to a better location on east Washington Street in downtown Summerville, and Bunton, having finished secretarial studies at North Georgia Business College, finally decided to work with me. Looking back at that time now, I realize that this was the best thing that ever happened to me during my long, erratic career.

But even though I had begun to settle down and try to live a more stable life... to work with Bunton and show her a little appreciation for the wonderful way she had raised both the girls and me... I still had one more foolish fling to go. I still wanted a real sea-worthy sailboat.

After much searching I found exactly what I wanted at a marina on the shores of Lake Lanier... a twenty three, (actually twenty six foot with appendage) Venture of Newport. Unlike the boxy landlubber craft to be found on most inland lakes today, the "Pondora", as we called her, sported a real nautical profile with curved gunnels, bowsprit, foresail and Yankee Jib.

Although Bunton had counseled against the venture, she traveled with me to Lanier and helped with loading and towing the boat back home. And when we finally got Pondora in the water at Weiss, she seemed to enjoy an afternoon from time to time sitting on the starboard cockpit lounge with a book and a glass of tea, while I worked to tack upstream from the Bay Spring Marina to the part of Weiss we had become familiar with before the Leaky Teki decided she was a submarine.

We were invited and joined the Rome Sailing club, and to my surprise Bunton seemed to enjoy going to the clubhouse and helping with preparations for the frequent dinner meetings and cookouts, as well as attending the periodic dinner meetings we had at selected restaurants in Rome. She quickly developed rapport with a number of ladies at the club, especially with Mary Ann, the pretty Swedish lady with a slight French accent... and I became engrossed with tales of adventure from some of the men who actually had experienced blue water sailing... something that I dearly wanted to do, but knew that I never would. Bunton, I knew would certainly draw the line at the dock if I should insist on taking the Pondora to a deep water port such as Panama City or Long Boat Key. And it was a sure thing that I would not go without her. I never had ventured far from home without her except for a few business trips, and I knew that I never would.

However, our lives at that time were probably as good, if not better than ever. The girls had moved back to our world, Jenette was in Birmingham, and Claudette and Jerry had come back to Georgia for Jerry to pastor the First Baptist church in Cedartown. This meant that we could see both our little girls often, as well as the two little boys, Jeremy and Terry who somehow had joined our clan.

Thanksgiving days, Christmas, birthdays, and anniversaries became wonderful times for the Ponder clan when all would come to Summerville and enjoy Grandmomma's famous turkey and dressing and all the other wonderful things she cooked. Although winter time, especially during the tax filing season required a little discipline, a time to make a little money... our summers were filled with trips to the beach, and long dream-filled days on the Pondora at Lake Weise.

However, a time is bound to come in all our lives that acts to change our often false perception of security. With me, it came one Saturday morning when the club was holding its annual racing event.

We were out tacking around outside the starting line, watching the members who were to participate in the race get in position. I sat for a moment listening to the flutter of the main sail, thinking I should round down and fasten the un-shackled boom vane. However, the luff was not loud enough to pry me from my comfortable position on the starboard seat.

I looked across at Bunton. She was sitting comfortably on the port-lounge, reading what must have been a pleasing saga from one of the many books she kept stashed aboard.

I smiled and marveled again at the youth that remained in the blue of her eyes. At times, I could still see in her the seventeen year-old girl I had married shortly after returning from the war. But now, as then, it was difficult for me to express the warm feeling she gave me at times like this. In fact, when she looked over at me, I turned away, hoping she would not see the emotion in my face, pretending to study the casual manner in which Ron was making sail in such a stiff wind.

I glanced back at the Bay Springs inlet, and then turned westward to observe the main body of the Regatta. I could see the profile of the Pegasus straining to brush her mast against the sun. The Desperado trailed in her wake, and others followed. I turned the boat slightly to port, aiming at the clubhouse, and bent on the tiller harness. The little cat's paws of the early morning were beginning to grow whiskers, and I felt a strong lift from the now gusty wind. I waited for a moment to see if the boat would track untended, adjusted the tiller slightly... waited a moment longer, and then went below.

While I had been in the cockpit, the wind had been gusty, but mainly from about 30 degrees. I had been confident that the condition would last until I returned topside. But suddenly, the wind shifted sharply. I felt the change just as I lifted a bottle from the ice-chest. Glancing up through the open hatch, I was amazed at the swift movement of the fluffy little cumulus clouds that had been drifting calmly by only a moment ago. Then, I realized that the gust had caught the vessel athwart ships, and the close-hauled sails were rolling her sharp alee.

I threw the bottle into the sink and raced to the ladder, but was forced to grab onto the hatch coaming and hold tightly as the mast-head reached for a drink of frosted water. Straining to push myself up the ladder, I looked over the coaming. Bunton was holding onto the cockpit rail, ready to plunge over the side. I tried to reach her, only to lose my footing and fall to the cabin sole. When I was back at the ladder, the boat started to right herself. I could still see Bunton's hand on the rail, and knew that she was safe. However, before I figured out what had happened... before I was aware that the boat had turned stern-to-wind and was about to jibe, the boom came over hard. I heard the deck-block snap against the stop, and almost fell up the ladder just as she started to heel in the other direction.

I reached out to Bunton, took her in my arms and almost fell overboard. And then I pushed her down, seated her in the empty lounge and told her to hold tightly to the rail as I took hold of the tiller and turned the Pondora back into the wind.

CHAPTER THIRTY FOUR

Over the next several years almost everything that happened seemed to enrich our lives. Jenette decided to add to the clan roster with a little boy called Reiner. Then she hit us with a double whammy... a couple of little sweetie-pies we call Bragan and Kilie. Unfortunately Claudette and Jerry decided to move several counties south about the same time Jenette and Coleman agreed to move to Georgia, where they settled for teaching jobs and bought a home at Armuchee, only a twenty minute drive from our home in Summerville.

By then I had given up all but the tax service segment of my accounting practice, and consequently we had much time to spare, especially during the summers... time to actually live the leisure life we had been accused of doing all along.

We still enjoyed the beach and usually made a trip or two south each summer and sometimes in the fall. However, by then Lake Weiss seemed to have lost its charm as well, so I arranged to live the second of the two most wonderful days of a sailor's life. According to legend, the first is the day one buys a sailboat, and the second is the day he sells it.

And then one day while Bunton was visiting with Jenette and the kids, Jenette called and told me that her mother had fallen on the driveway and bruised her face around her left eye.

"We're on our way to the emergency room, but I don't think it's very serious. No need for you to come, Daddy. I'll call you as soon as we see a doctor. I just thought we ought to have it looked at."

About an hour and forty five minutes later she called and said that the emergency room doctor, after having looked at the x-rays, didn't think it was serious. He placed a small bandage on the spot and they left and stopped at Applebee's for lunch... and then, Bunton drove home.

However, the next afternoon Dr. Joe Herron, her regular doctor, called and said that, although the fall didn't seem to have caused any serious damage, the x-rays showed a small shadow which he felt should be further examined. He said that he could simply take additional x-rays, but what he recommended was that she have a scan done at Rome Radiology. Consequently, he advised that he had made an appointment for her at 10 o'clock the next morning. He said that he was referring the case to neurosurgeon, Dr. Dennis Murphy, and that Dr. Murphy could see her at 2 o'clock the next day.

The next morning we went to Rome Radiology for the scan... had an early lunch at Applebee's, killed some time at the mall, and then went to Dr. Murphy's office on North 5th Avenue.

After several minutes waiting in the examination room, the door opened and Dr. Murphy came into the room. I almost fell from the hard little metal chair where I sat. "Son offal..." I almost whispered. I thought Willie Nelson had just entered the room. The man's hair was hanging almost to his waist in a loosely platted tangle... he was wearing blue jeans with buckskin shirt and scuffed-up cowboy boots. He put out his hand in greeting.

"I'm Dr. Murphy," he ventured, as he pulled out the little stool and sat down.

"Well young lady," he said, "looks like we have a little problem."

I was watching closely as the man opened a folder and removed some papers, while swiping at a strand of hair that had separated from the tangle atop his head to fall across his left eye. Bunton was watching me, hoping no doubt that I would not wash the man with a spray of sarcasm, as was my custom in situations such as this.

Then the cowboy doctor turned and handed both of us a picture.

"This!" he said. "This is called a 'cerebral aneurysm'... Boy!" He shook his head. "Boy, you've got a doozy."

The pictures were computer enhanced versions of shots produced by the new MRI machines. They showed a massive tangle of arteries with three ballooned-out sections. I understood what a cerebral aneurysm was, even if I had never seen a picture of one. My mother had died of that condition at the early age of 53. Unfortunately, at that time, the doctors at what was jokingly known as the "First aid Hospital" in Summerville, Georgia where she was carried probably didn't know much more about the disease than I did.

Murphy handed us another picture showing the thing from a different angle, and started to put the papers and pictures back inside the folder.

"I want you to go over to Birmingham and show this thing to Dr. Winfield Fisher. I'm sure that he will want to operate on this thing right away."

"Can't you do it?" Bunton asked. This was her way of showing respect to the man, even though I am sure she knew that there was no way I was going to let that tracker put a bone-saw to her scalp.

"Yes, I could!" he answered. "I do a few tumors from time to time and I worked on one cerebral aneurysm back in January. It was not a very complicated one. But when I talked to Dr. Fisher a couple of weeks ago, he had already operated on one hundred and forty two this year alone. Dr. Fisher is a world renowned neurosurgeon... he gets patients from all over the world. Now, you tell me... who do you want to do yours?"

About this time, I was ready to show a little respect for this 'sheep in wolves clothing' doctor. I always respected anybody who recognized and admitted his limitations. And I could see that Bunton was ready to head for Birmingham as well.

We arrived at the UAB facility on Thursday of the following week, and sat for only a few minutes in the examination room waiting for Dr. Fisher. He entered the room, shook hands with both of us, sat down on the little stool next to the examination table and opened a folder which contained the report and pictures Dr. Murphy had sent.

"I see you have met my friend, Dennis Murphy." He said. When neither of us spoke, he continued.

"Dennis is a little unusual," he ventured... "but he's on his way to becoming a great neurosurgeon." He looked at one of the papers and then picked up the pictures.

"This is an unusual aneurysm." he almost whispered. "I want to get our people to scan this thing first, and then we'll sit down and talk some more." He pressed a button on the wall by the lavatory, and a nurse came into the room.

"Take Mrs. Ponder down and tell Wilson we want 3d's," he said, and then turning to Bunton and me, "Go have a nice lunch... come back at two, and we'll try to figure out what to do."

When we returned after lunch, Dr. Fisher sat for a long time studying the radiology report and pictures, and then he handed each of us a picture and said, "I don't want to frighten you... I don't think this thing is about to start leaking right away, but Dr. Murphy was right. It is a very unusual aneurism." He turned his head sideways and looked at one of the pictures. "Whew"... he said. "I've seen a lot of these things, but I don't think I have ever seen one like this. Look at this," he continued, handing the picture to me. "Looks like some landlubber tried to tie a Bight knot on a Bowline. Whew!"

He took the picture back and put it in the folder with the other papers, and asked Bunton to sit on the examination table. Then, when he had examined the little bruise she got when she fell on the pavement and wrote some notes in the file, he said that he wanted to study the aneurism for a while before making a decision about the operation. "It's obvious that we will have to fix it," he said, "But I want to wait a while and see if there are any changes. I don't think there is any danger at the present time. It appears to me that all three of the little sacs in there are still in good shape. They look rather strong and somewhat thick. When one of them puffs out like a balloon and begins to look really thin is when we get excited and try to fix it."

He stood up and shook hands with both of us. "Stop at the check-out counter and I'll have them set up an appointment. Can you come back in about four weeks?"

CHAPTER THIRTY FIVE

We went back to Birmingham near the end of the next month, had the scans made and waited for Dr. Fisher in the examination room. He looked at the pictures, scratched his head and after a few minutes of conversation said that he would see us again in about three months.

In the meantime we, our whole family and friends, spent much time worrying. My mother had died from a cerebral aneurysm, and it seemed that everywhere we turned somebody had lost a loved one from the strange malady. I tried not to talk about it in Bunton's presence and advised the girls to caution. However, I could see that she had it on her mind most of the time.

At the end of the three months period we went back for our third appointment with Dr. Fisher. We drove into Birmingham in the middle of a horrific rainstorm and I found myself unable to see the road before me. At the same time large trucks rushed by our car seemingly only inches away, and a number of drivers blew their horns, leaving me to wonder if I was traveling on the wrong side of the road. Finally, when I was able to discern an off ramp, due mainly to the yellow line on the pavement, I turned on the emergency lights and eased off the main road where I waited impatiently for the rain to stop. However, it seemed that there was no end to our situation, so as soon as I could get up the nerve, I eased back out into the traffic and found my way to the UAB hospital downtown.

This time we had to wait for about an hour for the MRI scan, and after a leisurely lunch, for another two hours to see the doctor. Finally Dr. Fisher came into the examination room holding a folder in one hand and a couple of pictures in the other.

"Hi there," he smiled. "How's Georgia today?"

"Dry and sunny when we left," I ventured.

He shook hands with both of us, sat down on the little stool, and thumbed through the remaining pictures from the folder. Then he handed the pictures to me. These shots had been computer enhanced just as the ones from the other two scans; however, they looked much more revealing. As a matter of fact, the images looked as if one could pick them up and feel the little tangle of veins in hand.

"There hasn't been any movement," he said. "Matter of fact, the measurements show exactly the same as they did in our first scan. I know," he continued, "that you want to get this thing behind you... and I do as well. But, truth is I'm not ready to work on it yet. I want to study the thing a little longer. I think we should do a couple of more scans and make sure that there are no little thin spots on the back side of one of the lobes."

This bothered me immensely, but I was determined not to discuss that in Bunton's presence. The man had told me on at least two occasions that he had never seen a cerebral aneurysm like the mass of tangled veins in her head. As a matter of fact, I was beginning to think that he doubted his own ability to perform a successful operation on such a complicated condition.

In any event there seemed nothing we could do but follow his advice. After all, the man had been recommended as the very best neurosurgeon available.

Over the next year we traveled to Birmingham several times for the tedious and expensive MRI scans and waited anxiously for Dr. Fisher to decide what to do about her condition. During that time it became obvious that Bunton was held in high esteem by a multitude of people... many of whom we had not even seen for years. She received cards, letters and phone calls from near and far, and many whom I had not considered as special friends stopped me on the street or called me on the phone to express their concern and extend their good wishes. In conservation most would recall some act of kindness she had shown them or someone they knew. Many would point out with obvious admiration the fact that she had, in addition to raising two beautiful, active and popular daughters while putting up with me at the same time... spent many thousands of hours helping and caring for her grandmother and other members of her maiden family.

And it was amazing to see the seemingly never-ending witnesses of prayers offered on her behalf.

Finally upon our umpteenth visit to Birmingham, Dr. Fisher announced that he was ready to operate. Operation prep procedures were completed and an appointment for the operation was set for seven o'clock Monday June 13th, 2005... her seventy-fifth birthday.

On the evening of June 12th... we, the entire Ponder clan and our pastor, the Reverend David Craven, headed to Birmingham where we had booked rooms at a Great Western motel near the hospital.

That evening after we finished our carry-out supper, Bragan and Kilie, our granddaughters, brought a huge birthday cake containing seventy-five candles into our room, and we had a jolly good time watching Bunton puff the candles out and singing 'Happy Birthday Grandmother.' However, the feeling of tinged-joy soon departed when all the family had left the room.

When Bunton had finished her bath and lay down on the bed, I sat by the bed and talked with her for a while. Then when it appeared that she was very sleepy, I excused myself and went out and stood on the balcony. A beautiful yellow moon stood up from behind a distant mountain and marched gracefully across the sky, but my mind was far from the beauty of the idyllic scene.

I remembered my mother's death and many similar stories told me in recent times of others who had lost loved ones from cerebral aneurysms. And thinking of my mother, I remembered how adamantly she had stuck to her belief that God would heal if asked with sincere conviction and Christian faith. Thinking back I also remembered many times when that phenomenon had been demonstrated to my own advantage. I remembered the time in France when, after the fact, I learned that my mother and father had been down on their knees praying for me at the very moment the Jeep I was riding in struck a building, turned upside down and fell to the ground with a pretty young girl and me snuggled safely beneath the up-turned front seat, while at the same time her mother was saying a prayer at the Catholic church near her home. And I remembered several other occasions when either a divine power or an awful lot of good luck had allowed me to reach a ripe old age... Such as the time I stalled that old 7A3 Champ about three hundred feet above the runway at the Rome airport, or the time I fell out of the motor boat on the Tennessee River at Guntersville Alabama and had the thing turn around and run over my frightened body. And there were many more, including but not limited to, some situations I managed to get myself into overseas.

But this was something I didn't want to leave to good luck. This was something in which I felt the need for a little help from the God in which my mother had so vehemently trusted. So setting aside the doubts I had kept locked inside my mind for so long, I went into the room, checked to see if she was asleep, and for the first time in ages, knelt by her bed and whispered a sincere prayer.

CHAPTER THIRTY SIX

When we arrived at the hospital the next morning, Bunton was rushed into the prep section of the operation area and we were directed to a waiting room. Then, after a few minutes a nurse came and said that two of us could go in and stay with her until time for the operation. Of course I was one of the first to go, and the girls took time about coming in for only a few moments at a time.

Finally, when she was rolled into the operating room, I returned to the waiting room to find three people sitting with our family who were not there earlier. One was our pastor David Craven, who had just arrived from his motel room, and another was Diane Whitson, a very close friend of our daughter, Jenette. The other was David Lucas, a friend of Coleman, our son-in-law. David and Coleman had attended Samford University together, had been members of the same church and close friends for a number of years. When he was introduced to me, David said that he and some friends had organized an international prayer chain and that e-mail letters had already gone out asking members to pray for Bunton at the very moment she was in the operating room. He said that the prayer chain members were very dedicated and that many would be on their knees around the world at that very moment. This caused me to think again about the Jeep wreck, and how my parents had been praying for me at that time. And I must admit that I joined with the others in silent prayer over the next several hours while she was in the operating room.

Finally, after about seven hours a nurse came to the waiting room and said that the operation went well, and that Dr. Fisher would be in to talk to us shortly... and then, after another thirty minutes or so of impatient waiting, Dr. Fisher came through the waiting room door looking very weary and tired.

"Well," he said. "I think that she's going to be alright. The operation took a little longer than I expected, but she came through if very well. However, I must tell you that there are no guarantees in a case like this. We had to keep the blood flow cut off longer at times than I like".

He went on to explain that it was necessary to clamp the main artery temporarily each time he worked to place a clamp around one of the several little protrusions that had deformed the artery leading into her brain.

"She now has seven little metal clamps in her head... that's a lot, but I feel that she will be OK."

"What is the most likely thing that could happen?" Claudette asked.

Dr. Fisher explained that this kind of operation, mainly due to the cessation of blood flow could cause several problems. "For example," he said, "things such as memory loss, speech problems, total or partial loss of sight, loss of hearing... and the list goes on. As a matter of fact, cerebral aneurysms often cause the same problems that strokes cause."

When he left the room we sat for a while dumbfounded, overjoyed that she had come through the operation, and then, allowing our minds to walk through the litany of problems the doctor had left us to ponder.

When she was out of recovery and placed in a room, we were allowed to go in and see her. And, although we were advised to visit in groups of two, and not to linger too long, we all finally wound up in her room. After a little quite conversation, preacher Craven said a prayer, and all but Claudette and I went back to the waiting room. Finally, after several visits by the twins and some of the boys, Claudette and Jenette persuaded me to return to the motel for a nap.

I guess it's fair to say that that nap turned out to be a restless one. I lay awake most of the time thinking back on all the times I had done things that hurt her. I wondered why the God she had loved and trusted all her life would allow her to suffer in such manner, while I... who had doubted him most of my life, was allowed to walk around strong and healthy. It's true that I had had my own aneurism, the abdominal kind. However, a young vascular surgeon in Rome had removed that monkey from my back with an AneuRx Endovascular Stent Graft almost without pain.

When I went back to the hospital and entered her room, Bunton smiled and motioned for me to come closer, and when I bent down and kissed her on the cheek, she whispered, "I wish... I wis' I" ... and I realized that she was unable to speak what was on her mind.

I thought of what the doctor had said.... "Things such as memory loss, speech problems, total or partial loss of sight, loss of hearing, and the list goes on."

Claudette came closer and stood with me and held her mother's hand and whispered... "She doesn't seem to be able to say what she's thinking. She's been trying to talk to us, but she never finishes what she wants to say."

"I heard what he... I ah." Bunton almost whispered. "I... ah heard him." Claudette pulled me aside.

"She's been referring to girls as he or him, and to boys as she. I think she's really confused."

CHAPTER THIRTY SEVEN

When we were able to carry her home, the confusion continued. It was obvious that her mind was working properly, but it seemed that she could never completely express what she was thinking. We called and talked to Dr. Fisher, and he said that he thought the problem would clear up within a short time. He said that this was one of the most common problems occurring with this kind of operation. "I'll call Dr. Murphy," he continued, "and have him arrange for a speech therapist and a physical therapist to see her."

The physical therapist came first and Bunton was ready to cancel that treatment almost before the first session was over. However, we talked her into continuing for a while. Then the speech therapist came and worked with her for over two hours. Bunton seemed to like this lady and asked her in her newly acquired manner of speech to come back soon. However, after a number of sessions with the therapist, she still was not able to complete a full sentence most of the time... and this caused her to actually cry with frustration. She would usually stop in the middle of a sentence, and say... "Just forget it."

This was very hard for me to see. Bunton had been so full of life… and we had grown so close together over the last several years. After she had come to work with me in the office some twenty or twenty-five years earlier, life for us had been just short of wonderful. With the children grown and out of the house, we both seemed to have taken a new look at life and realized once again the wonderful gift God had given that day in the little grocery store on Commerce street when Mary Jim introduced her to me… "This is my friend, Mary Frances Gilmer" I remembered. "Everybody calls her Bunton."

But now, that that same God had allowed part of the gift he had given to diminish… my doubts or to put it another way, my inability to understand his divine plan, returned causing me once again to question his very existence.

However, this was not something I discussed with Bunton, or with anyone else for that matter. Nonetheless, my mind kept asking the same, seemingly unanswerable question… "Why would a loving God punish one of his most faithful subjects, when he had promised in his own word to do otherwise?"

Example Exodus 15:26: *"If thou wilt diligently hearken to the voice of the Lord thy God, and wilt do that which is right in his sight, and wilt give ear to his commandments, and keep all his statutes, I will put none of these diseases upon thee, which I have brought upon the Egyptians: for I am the Lord that healeth thee."*

I remembered my mother. My mother had been one of the most devoted Christians in the world. I cannot remember a time when I was at home that my mother went to bed without getting down on her knees in prayer. I doubt that she ever sat down at the table to eat without asking God's blessing… and I know without a doubt that she trusted and believed that God would heal her simply because he had promised. But she too had always seemed to be the one who suffered. As a matter of fact, she had suffered an early death from the same thing Bunton was afflicted with… a cerebral aneurysm.

However, as time passed Bunton's speech problem seemed to diminish. Or perhaps I was simply learning to anticipate what she was trying to say and somehow convey to her the fact that I understood. In any event, she seemed to be able to carry on a conversation without becoming frustrated and giving up with, "Just forget it." As a matter of fact, she seemed to enjoy talking, especially when we would meet someone she had not seen for a while. And fortunately, friends would stop and talk to her in a mall or one of the restaurants we frequently visited and never seem to notice when she was unable to complete a sentence. And to look at her, one would be hard-pressed to believe that she had ever suffered bad health. As a matter of fact, for a lady of seventy-five plus, she was still more beautiful than most gals half her age.

To prove that point, I am having a picture of her placed on the back cover of this book which was taken about a year later when she was seventy-six.

As I sit here before my little keyboard writing these words, my mind races back over the years to bring back a kaleidoscope of images... images of her when she was young. It's amazing how memory can capture a picture and hold it for eons and give it back to you totally intact. The picture I now see is that of a beautiful twenty-four year old girl standing in the middle of the street before our little house on South Edmonson Street. She stands with hands on hips offering a half smile and an unspoken question... "What now?"

The "What Now" that she was about to ask was related to the pretty little palomino pony I was leading up the street.

The day before, we had passed Mr. Jackson's house at the foot of the hill where South Edmonson Street enters Highway 27. This was the first time the girls, Claudette and Jenette, had noticed what Mr. Jackson was doing with the large field between his house and the river. However, I had stopped there on several occasions and looked at the little herd of ponies Mr. Jackson was beginning to accumulate. As a matter of fact, I had inquired about the cost of one of the beautiful little animals and decided that my little girls didn't want one. But that notion was put to rest that day when I mistakenly drove down to the end of South Edmonson Street.

"Oh, look Daddy...look Daddy! Look at the pretty horses. Look Mommy... oh Daddy, can we have one?"

"Come on now! You're not cowgirls. You're just a couple of little sweetie pies. You are not big enough to ride horses."

"Yes we are Daddy... yes we are. Tell him Mommy. Tell him we can ride. Oh please Daddy... please. Can we get one?"

"I don't think we can afford a horse right now." Bunton said, "Horses cost a lot of money."

"Daddy's got lots of money!" Claudette ventured. Bunton smiled. She didn't know that I had saved over three hundred-fifty dollars over the last several months.

"Daddy's trying to save money to buy an airplane." I said... and this was the truth. I had not talked to Bunton about my plan yet, and if you were not around trying to support a family in February of 1955, you probably want believe that one could buy a pretty good old J3 Cub... a 7A3 Champ, or maybe even a well-used Luscombe for around six hundred dollars at that time.

That night when the subject came up again, as it was bound to do, Jenette said... "You can get a airplane Daddy. We don't hafta get a horse."

Well, as you might know, that sealed the deal. The little palomino I was leading up the street would be the closest thing to an airplane I would be able to buy for a long time to come.

When I came to where Bunton and the girls stood waiting at the end of our walk, (we would not allow them to enter the street) Bunton turned the mischievous look into the words I knew she would ask, "What now?" and I told her about my huge savings account.

"Well, where are you going to keep it?"

I told her about the arrangement Mr. Jackson had made, and she seemed pleased, although she would not put such pleasure into words. I think she was more worried that the girls might be hurt by the animal than about the money.

As a matter of fact, she almost didn't even have that to worry about. Mr. Jackson had almost not allowed me to buy the little horse he called "Pogo." I had approached him about the purchase without even arranging for a place to keep the animal. However, he went inside and called Mrs. McWhorter who lived across the street from us and arranged for me to place Pogo in her fence with the beautiful, large sheep she had.

Finally, after the girls had ridden Pogo bareback with both Bunton and me holding on to them each step of the way, we carried the little horse across the street and placed him in the fence with Mrs. McWhorter's sheep.

"What did you pay?" Bunton asked when we were finally alone.

"Two Hundred," I almost whispered.

"Two hundred?" She said startled. "Henderson! That would buy a new living room suite."

Well, the next morning I went to the bank and withdrew the remainder of my secrete hoard and gave it to Bunton, and today, April 24th, 2013 I can still feel the wonderful bonding emotion that passed between us... the understanding that love was more important than ponies, airplanes, and even living room suites.

CHAPTER THIRTY EIGHT

As time passed, the speech problem seemed to diminish and Bunton did not appear to get so upset when she would occasionally have a problem with forming all the words she needed to carry on normal conversation. We started to go out in public more often, especially in the evenings when we would drive to Rome for dinner at one of the many good restaurants that seemed to be popping up all over town.

Of course, we did not go on long trips the way we used to do, but with Jenette and Coleman now living only twenty minutes away at Armuchee, we found plenty of places to visit, both together with them and alone.

By Thanksgiving that year, Bunton seemed to be almost back to normal, and that was great news to the whole family. We had been used to enjoying the greatest cooking in the world, especially on Thanksgiving and Christmas days. And, as you know, good food goes great with football.

That Thanksgiving Day started just like any other Thanksgiving Day at our house. The kids that arrived the day and night before were up and around almost before the sleep genie pried my eyelids apart... and before the breakfast dishes were washed, both the living room and the den looked like the aftermath of a hippy pajama party.

Bunton went about preparing the Thanksgiving meal that day as she always did when the kids were home... with a look of sheer delight. And the girls as usual were busy helping. As a matter of fact, it seemed that none of us remembered the horrible experience we had gone through only a short time ago, until we sat down to eat and Kilie was chosen to ask the blessing.

"Dear God, thank you for this food, and for our family, and especially for allowing Grandmother to share this Thanksgiving Day with us." At that point in time, the neuron activity in the Hippocampus cortex of my brain must have stopped. I cannot remember another word Kilie said. But today the words, "especially for allowing Grandmother to share this Thanksgiving day with us" rings clear in my mind as I remember the quiet, and almost overpowering feeling of thankfulness that seemed to hold us together during that most memorable Thanksgiving dinner.

Thinking back on that day, it's hard not to recall other days... many other special days when we were together as a family unit, days when Bunton's love and devotion held us in a tight invisible embrace.

Although showing more humor than family devotion, another time when one of the grandkids asked the blessing comes to mind. At that time, we had only two grandchildren... two full-of-spunk little fellows who never seemed to agree on anything. It had already been established that when visiting our house, Jeremy, the oldest would ask the blessing on one occasion, and Terry the next. On that occasion when the turkey and all us people were properly seated at the table... after a few minutes of discussion between the little guys, we bowed our heads and held hands as Terry did the honors.

"Thank you Jesus for this good food and for letting us come and eat at Grandmother's house and bless Mommy and Daddy and me and Jeremy and Aunt Jenette and Uncle Coleman and Granddaddy and even Grandmother."

It is times like these that bring a rush of unforgettable images of our little clutch hovered together around that table enjoying the fruits of Bunton's labor. And it is obvious that all the clan loved her for much more than the delicious entrees she prepared. As a matter of fact, I guess I sometimes felt a little pang of jealously because I was not always the center of attraction.

In the fall of that year, the year of her operation, Leonard and Betty Parker, our dearest friends from Columbus, Georgia came to visit us. Leonard and I were very close boyhood friends. We had the same interest, especially that of thumping on the old guitar, and our dreams of someday becoming great country and western stars were probably just about the same. At some time before we both joined the army, Leonard's family moved to Columbus, Georgia and he came to live with us. And then after the war when we were both back at home, he came back and stayed with us until Bunton and I were married in December of 1947. And you might guess after all these years of visiting back and forth, and of visiting many places of attraction, from the white sand beaches of Florida to the Great Smoky Mountains together, that Bunton was glad to see them come.

I don't remember exactly where we went during that visit, except that we enjoyed as we always did the time together. And I can remember that Bunton mentioned the visit on several occasions over the next year or so.

CHAPTER THIRTY NINE

Over the next several months it became obvious that the operation had caused more damage than first thought. Not only did the speech problem start to manifest itself more noticeably, we learned that she was losing her ability to do certain little things such as look up a number and dial the telephone. Consequently, I arranged to have a Philips Lifeline medical alert system installed only to learn that she would not push the call button when I asked. She would say, "That's just a bunch of foolishness... I'll call you if I want to." But the fact was she couldn't. So, I decided to trim my client list even more than I had over the last few years, and arrange for only one or two appointments daily. This way, when the tax filing season arrived in January, I could see that she had everything she needed for a late sleep in the morning, go to the office for a quick interview and bring the file back home where I would complete preparing the client's tax return.

This worked well until about the end of the '06 filing season in April of 2007. I would get up early and see that she finished her toilet, at which time I would have our breakfast ready... two tall glasses of instant breakfast, sometimes with ice-cream. On many occasions, one of our little sweetie-pies,

Bragan or Kelie would stay over and take care of Grandmother. They loved her very much. However, early in May when Bunton went in for her annual Mammogram, our world turned upside down again. The diagnosis was breast cancer.

She was referred to Dr. Paul Brock, a surgeon at the Harbin Clinic in Rome, Georgia. And when the operation occurred, as we had expected from several sources of information, Dr. Brock insisted on doing a full-blown Mastectomy.

It was very hard for me to understand when Bunton seemed to be totally indifferent about the prospect of such an operation. I wondered if she simply didn't understand what was about to happen... how could she be so nonchalant? Had she simply just given up... succumbed to her fate? She had always had so much pride, and rightly so. Few women at her age could still turn heads the way she could. And I knew in my heart that Bunton was suffering from much more than the physical pain she surely felt.

As for myself... well, you might have guessed already that my doubts about God's divine plan... about his promise, *"If thou wilt diligently hearken to the voice of the Lord thy God, I will put none of these diseases upon thee,"* had returned to haunt me.

I felt sure that if that preacher at the Church of God in Berryton Georgia was still around, I would go down and punch him in the mouth for all the lies he had told me. I was totally convinced, as when I was a little boy, that he was more

174

interested in momma's fried chicken than in the condition of her health, or the salvation of her soul. However, I am fully aware that ministerial hypocrisy did not start with that preacher. As a matter of fact, I have no evidence that he was not a devoted Christian with total faith in what he preached and the way he lived.

On the other hand, it is obvious that there are men-of-the-cloth whose inclusion in the ministry serves only to disgrace the profession. Think of all those television preachers who spend their entire air time trying to convince you that sending them a generous contribution will serve as a down payment on a mansion in Heaven... and there are others who actually commit despicable, criminal acts. For example, our own Miles Phillips, former pastor of the South Summerville Baptist Church, served time in prison for child molestation.

All these men claimed to be men of God. They claimed that God spoke to them and guided them in the faith... and I was not surprised that some may have fallen short of righteous, because due to my reversion to a childhood mentality, I was ready to believe that God's own word was often misleading.

In any event, there was more to worry about than trying to figure out God's plan. Men much smarter than I, have spent lifetimes trying to do that. My job was to see that Bunton had everything I could provide to make her comfortable, and try to give her reason to live... reason to carry on with life, and I knew that I would have to do better than I had in the past.

However, she did not seem to suffer from depression after the operation, as I had thought she would. It turned out that the hospital provided excellent recovery services, including a department dedicated to counseling post-op breast cancer patients. The department was headed by a wonderful nurse who had suffered double Mastectomy operations herself. She visited with Bunton several times and helped with selecting all the paraphernalia she would need to make her look and feel like the beautiful lady she was.

We were also helped very much by our daughters. Jenette now lived only about twenty minutes away at Armuchee, and although Claudette was living in Moultrie, Georgia… a good six to seven hour drive away, she came often. And of course, the sweetie-pies were in and out almost every day.

As it turned out, Bunton was quite nonchalant about the operation, as she had been when first diagnosed. As a matter of fact, it wasn't very long until we were going out to eat and visiting almost as often as before.

CHAPTER FORTY

Things went very well during the remainder of 2007 and the big part of 2008. Bunton seemed to have accepted the outcome of the mastectomy as she finally had accepted the speech problem caused by the aneurism. As a matter of fact she even made several shopping trips with Jenette and Claudette on occasions when Claudette came to visit.

When Thanksgiving came that year, 2008, all our family came home as usual. Of course, that year Jenette and Coleman and their children were already close by. As I have stated before, Jenette and Coleman had returned to Georgia and accepted teaching positions in the Floyd county school system at Armuchee. Their daughter Bragan was at the University of Alabama at Tuscaloosa which is only a short drive, and Reiner and Kilie were both at home in Armuchee pursuing their educations at schools within driving distance.

Of course Claudette, Jerry and Jeremy had a rather long drive up from Moultrie in South Georgia; Jeremy lived only about two blocks from his parents in Moultrie. Terry and Mary Ann along with the great-grand's, Luke, Kate and Taylor lived only about two hours' drive away at Carrolton.

That Thanksgiving Day the girls prepared most of the food... something that Bunton would not usually allow. Of course, she was granted the right to cook a couple of her famous cakes, with a little help from Bragan the second best cook in town. By that time, we had persuaded Bunton to buy the bird already cooked, and although there were about nine or ten wild turkeys grazing in our yard that morning, our dinner guest came to us from Ingles Grocery store with his toes already turned up to cool.

Although our holidays were always joyful occasions, I would venture to say that this was the best Thanksgiving Day we had ever shared. The games were good, but sometimes overshadowed and drowned out by claps and screams, as the world's greatest sports fans tried to tell the players exactly how to handle the ball. However, when the dinner bell rang, the televisions were turned up to about 150 decibels and we all gathered around in a great circle between the table in the dining room and the extra one in the living room, and held hands.

It turned out that it was Terry's time to say the blessing, and the quiet sound of his words could be heard clearly over the roaring clatter of the TV sets.

"Dear God! You have blessed us once again with the opportunity to be here together in this place we all love. You have given us another chance to be here with Grandmother and Granddaddy and with each other to share this bounty of wonderful food which you have provided. Thank you God for allowing this union, and thank you especially for allowing us to share this wonderful day with Grandmother and Granddaddy once again. Bless this food to the nourishment of our bodies, and go with us to our respective homes where we shall remember this day forever."

At that time chairs scraped across hardwood floors, causing Bunton to shake her head in that, "There goes my beautiful floor again" expression, and a giggle from the sweetie pies, and the jingle of silverware, the clatter of plates, and the rumble of voices brought back many memories to overshadow the roar of the far-away voices that sought to spoil our happy celebration.

Shortly after Thanksgiving that year Kilie had a few days off from school and decided to spend them with us. This was wonderful. It is always a pleasure to have one of the kids around. It was particularly good having Kilie with us that time. This gave me a little time to get out and do some things I needed to do. Consequently, on the second morning after she arrived, I left early and drove up to the Wal-Mart store at Trion to look for a couple of items I had been thinking about buying. Just before I left, Kilie came to our bedroom with breakfast for Bunton and herself, teasing me that I should go to Jim's restaurant and have breakfast at the 'Liars Table'. And, I did.

However, almost as soon as I arrived at Wall-Mart I received a call from Philips Lifeline medical alert service telling me that I should go home at once. "Your wife is sick. Your granddaughter is with her, and we have already called 911.

Please be careful driving... we will stay in touch at your home until both you and the ambulance arrives."

"Dear Jesus! What now? What else is going to happen to her?" I did not use the caution that Lifeline recommended. It is only about three and a half miles from Wall-Mart to our home... I turned that space into about a two minute drive. The Ambulance station is only three-quarters of a mile from home, but I beat them there by at least five minutes.

When I arrived, Bunton was on the bed in the guest room where Kilie had slept. She was gasping for breath with a wheezing sound and a gurgle in her throat. Kilie was handling the situation like a trained nurse. She had already checked her pulse, her temperature and blood pressure. She started in to instruct me on what to do, and I helped her get Bunton up on the side of the bed and slipped her robe on as we waited for the medics to arrive.

"Dear God!" I stammered. "What are you doing to her now?" I was certain that God had decided to visit every vile disease he could conjure upon her just to prove that he was in charge.

And then, the ambulance arrived and the medics rushed her outside, shoved her into the thing and allowed me to sit in the front seat with the driver where I could scarcely see her through a small opening behind the seats. Kilie followed, bringing all the things she thought necessary... calling Jenette and everybody else in the family she could reach as she drove.

When we arrived at the hospital, Jenette and Coleman were already there waiting. Reiner came shortly thereafter, Bragan started her journey from Tuscaloosa, and within a very short time, Claudette started her long drive from Moultrie, in South Georgia.

The Redmond Regional Hospital served us well that day. Bunton was rolled into a treatment room right away where doctors and nurses started to work to save her life. She was rushed to another part of the hospital where fluid was drawn from her lungs and other necessary measures taken. And then finally, a doctor came to the waiting area and advised us that she was O.K.

"Your mother," he said to Jenette, "has suffered a severe congestive heart failure. It is very fortunate that you got her here when you did."

CHAPTER FORTY ONE

When we were able to carry her home that time, we decided to stay with Jenette and Coleman. We moved back into the rooms they had provided for us earlier and settled in for the remainder of the winter. As a matter of fact, we stayed there until after the 2008 tax season which ended in April 2009. This allowed me to drive to Summerville to my office in the mornings, leaving either Kilie or Bragan to care for Bunton. The drive was only about twenty minutes away and I knew that I could be back with her quickly if anything happened.

In the meantime, our local Home Health Care service brought in equipment which allowed us to check all her vital signs each morning and have them transmitted via phone line to the HHC office.

I was really surprised that things went so well. Bunton seemed to come around and be more herself after the heart attack, than before. Her speech problem improved, and soon she was able to go out and eat, something she dearly loved to do. We would drive over to Calhoun, or Ringgold, or some other nearby location and have dinner at one of her favorite restaurants... the Cracker Barrel.

When the tax season was finally over, we moved back to our home in Summerville, and I made arrangements to close my downtown office and open a small one at home. I cleared out a little storage room on the back side of our carport and moved in. This would allow me to be with her almost twenty-four seven. To augment my plan, I rigged the office with both visual and audio monitoring equipment and placed motion detection devises in the bedroom to alert me if she should get out of bed quietly when I was not watching the visual monitor. It's true that she was much better... that she could carry on a conversation of sorts with me now, but another problem had ensued. She had recently developed a severe problem with a condition commonly known as vertigo, and this required that someone be with her at all times when she was on her feet.

As you might have guessed this constant togetherness and the fact that she needed my care now more than ever before taught me to think about her and her well-being in a different light. It made me think about all the things she had done for me... about the gift of love she had given me all those years ago when I needed it the most, and it brought us closer together in a spiritual sense than we had ever been before.

It's amazing how one's entire outlook on life can change almost overnight. Up until this time I was constantly looking forward... hoping to accomplish things I had always wanted to do. And now, all I wanted was to live a normal life... to bring a modicum of pleasure to the girl who had given me so much love and devotion for so many years. It became a sheer pleasure just to get her in the car and drive to Rome for a quiet dinner. I hungered for the times when we used to spend long evenings together sitting on the beautiful white sand beaches of Long Boat Key, and I could almost see a whisk of cloud drifting over the mountains at Helen... or hear the flutter of sails in the wind at Lake Weiss .

However, fate had not yet finished with me and my girl. On a Thursday afternoon in June that year, Bunton decided she wanted to take a little ride. I helped her out, into the car, and thank God, made sure that her seat-belt was securely fastened. And then, when I got behind the wheel and started the engine she reminded me that I had not locked the house doors.

"It won't matter... we'll be back in a few minutes." I said.

"No! I don't want to leave it open. Go lock it. Go lock it."

Then just as I placed the key into the front door lock, I heard a bump and a scrape and turned to see the car dip over the small embankment at the end of the pavement and crush through the little split-rail fence... and my heart almost failed as the thing started to roll down into the deep ravine that separates our house from Hammond Drive.

"Dear God," I screamed, "Dear God, what now" as I raced to the edge of the pavement and jumped over the embankment to chase after the car. "Dear Jesus"... but I could not blame God or Jesus for this tragedy. God had given me a brain and taught me how to use it, but I had failed to listen.

"Dear God!" I continued to scream as I hooked my foot into a tangle of vines and fell head-long to the ground. And then I got to my feet and raced off down the hill as hard as I could run, only to fall again and again.

When I got to the car at the bottom of the ravine, she was sitting quietly looking a little confused. I tried to open the door, only to learn that it was jammed tight. As the car rolled down the hill, the driver's side door which was standing open when I left, slammed into a tree and bounced the car to the right into another tree, and then it bounced back in the other direction and back again. And this bouncing from tree to tree is probably responsible for saving her life, because by the time the car reached the bottom of the ravine, the bouncing from tree to tree had slowed it down just before it came to rest against a large oak at the very bottom.

By the time the EMT got to us, I had managed to pry the driver's side door open and crawl inside and undo her seat belt. I helped her to the driver's side and held her in my arms until help arrived.

When we returned home from the Redmond emergency room, I stood for a long time looking down into the ravine. I stood dumbfounded as I looked back at the parking area where I had planned to place a curb almost twenty-eight years ago when we built the house. The rails from the little split-rail fence were scattered on the ground and I realized that I had used that little fence as a child uses a security blanket. I had felt secure with my car pulled up close to the thing, when I should have known that it would not hold the weight of a large car. I looked back down the hill. My beautiful pearl-white Cadillac lay there at the bottom of the ravine... now an ugly pile of pearl-white junk.

"Dear God!" I whispered again. "How could I have been so stupid?"

CHAPTER FORTY TWO

In November, 2010, Claudette and Jerry moved back to Summerville. Jerry had resigned as pastor of the Moultrie First Baptist church some time earlier and had taken a position as special assistant to the president for church relations with Mercer University where he already served on the board. And now to our pleasant surprise, they had decided to come back and pastor the Horizon Baptist Fellowship in Summerville... our other little baby girl was coming home.

Things had gone much better with Bunton after she recovered from the heart problem. She had had some health problems to be sure, but most of the problems were from common illnesses which didn't bring about the anxiety we all had suffered due to the aneurism, cancer and heart failure. As a matter of fact, I think we began to feel that things were back to normal again. We enjoyed a wonderful Christmas holiday that year and Bunton and I attended church services several times in early 2011... something we had not done for some time now.

With Claudette back, she and Jenette as well as the sweetie pies spent much time with Bunton, leaving me free to do some things that I had not been able to do earlier. I spent much time working on my on-line magazine, the Chattooga Camera, which I had launched about two years earlier, and I toyed with the idea of writing another book... but the inspirational juices did not flow, so consequently I wound up just hanging around the house when I was not busy with a client in the office.

It's amazing how easy it is to fall back into a state of indifference... a state of nonchalance when one feels secure and sure that the danger has passed. And that, I guess, is what happened to me when I was once again able to come and go as I pleased. Bunton seemed to be almost back to her old self... back to a time when she enjoyed life a little... life without pain and suffering. However, as the old saying goes... "It's not a good idea to count your chickens before they hatch".

That spring when she went in for her annual mammogram, she and Claudette came back home with the worst kind of news.

"Momma's got cancer again," Claudette almost whispered when we were alone together. "She has a small lump in the same side. The doctor did a biopsy, and he said he was sure it was cancer. We'll know for sure when the report comes back next week." She started to cry.

I went outside... out to my office where I sat for a long time and whispered all the things I had told God the other time... and the scripture came back to haunt me.

"If you listen carefully to the voice of the Lord your God and do what is right in his eyes, I will not bring on you any of the diseases I brought on the Egyptians."

"Well!" I thought. "Bunton has come as close to doing that as anybody I know, and look how you have treated her."

I was livid… almost full of hate. I could not understand why it always had to be her that suffered. "Why not me?" I almost cried. "Why does a sorry rascal like me go through life without a scratch, while a person such as Bunton… such as my mother… people who have spent their entire life doing everything by the book, why do you make them suffer. Is there anything about your scripture that is truthful? Can I believe anything about God and the scriptures my parents used to read to me every night?"

CHAPTER FORTY THREE

The doctor who did the biopsy was right. The pathology report showed that she had a small malignancy in the same side where the mastectomy was performed. When she went in for the operation, Dr. Brock claimed that this was a different kind of cancer. He had been adamant that he had removed all traces of the other cancer which did not require radiation. This time, he averred that radiation would be required with this kind of cancer. I was not sure that this was not a ruse to cover the fact that he had not entirely removed the first tumor.

In any event, this still attractive eighty-one year old girl who had never harmed a living creature went under the doctor's knife yet another time. And this old man who has never commenced to do the good she had done, suffered only for the pain she felt.

However, the aftermath of this operation went better in many ways than the times before. This no doubt was because Claudette was back home now to help with all the chores required of a family in times like this. She came to the house almost daily and carried her mother to Rome for most of the radiation treatments.

During the remainder of 2011 and through the summer of 2012, Bunton's health seemed to improve. Her speech problem abated to a point where she seemed anxious for conversation. She would stop people whom I did not even recognize and talk as if she and that person were the best of friends. And after listening to them chat, I would often realize that they were indeed long time acquaintances.

However, around the end of August things started to turn in the other direction. The vertigo returned, causing her to fall backwards when she stood up. This meant that someone had to be with her each time she stood... each time she went to the bathroom, which was often. The speech problem also returned. This time not only could she not put her thoughts into words... it seemed that she was becoming totally confused, unable to think intelligently... unable to remember where she was, and what she was doing.

I would carry her out onto the front porch and sit with her and we would talk. She seemed satisfied that I could understand the broken sentences she spoke, and it was clear that she understood me. And then, after a moment of silence, she would look at me and ask,

"Where are we?"

"We're at home." I would answer.

"Yes, but where?"

"We're at our house on the side of the hill. Look!" I would point down the hill to the other side of the ravine and say. "Look! That's Charlotte's house. You remember Charlotte don't you?"

At that her expression would change and the look of bewilderment would vanish.

"Yes, I remember. But she's gone. She's not there anymore."

By mid-September she was almost totally comatose. It was necessary that I or one of the girls be with her all the time. Her problem with incontinence grew worse, and she needed to go to the bathroom very often, sometimes eight or ten times during the night.

Between the girls and the sweetie-pies Bragan and Kilie, I was still able to go to the park or sit on the shores of Sloppy Floyd Lake for a couple of hours during the daytime. However, at night, due to the fact that the kids were living very busy lives... working, going to school and all the other things necessary to keep the wheels of life in motion, I was left to care for her through the nights. And this was what I wanted. She needed me to hold her, to cuddle her, and to whisper words of encouragement through the darkness of night and the wee hours of morning.

At times we would go out onto the porch late into the night... sometimes in the early mornings, long before the neighborhood rooster chased the sleep genie from his roost and proclaimed his mastery of the animal domain... and Bunton would invariably ask,

"Where are we?"

Her trips to the bathroom increased, and sometimes it was almost impossible for me to jump up, go around and take hold of her before she was totally out of bed. On two occasions she actually fell. Fortunately, I was able to grab on and hold her to the best of my ability as she slid to the floor... and both times it was necessary for me to call 911 for help in getting her up and back in bed.

Towards the very end of September she virtually stopped eating. When I would carry in a tall glass of instant breakfast, something she had always loved... she would push me away saying, "Don't want. Don't want."

Her doctor, Dr. Joseph Herron, decided that we needed special help and asked the director of the Hospice service at Floyd Medical Center to come and see us. On their first visit, Bunton sat on the living room couch and talked to the social director almost as if she had never had a health problem in her life.

However, after seeing her again, Dr. Herron asked that Hospice service be instituted... consequently the social director and a nurse came back for another interview. This time it was obvious that their care was sorely needed, and all the paperwork was done for Hospice care to commence. The Hospice nurses and other workers came and brought equipment and supplies needed for their purpose.

Then on October 4th 2012 at about four-thirty in the morning, she went to the bathroom for what I think was the eleventh time that night. I held onto her precariously, sat on the little folding chair in a sleepy daze for what seemed hours, and staggeringly led her back and helped her into bed. And then, just as I managed to lie down and pull the covers over my sleepy body, she rolled over and started to climb out of bed.

"I've got to go!" She chanted. "Got to go... got to go."

"Dear God, no!" I almost screamed. "No, no, no. You just went. Get back in bed," I shouted as I grabbed onto her and pushed her in the direction of the bed. "Get back in."

"Going to porch!" she cried. "Going to porch!"

I held her with brute force and pushed her towards the bed. "We can't go to the porch," I said... trying to calm my voice. "We can't go to the porch... it's cold and raining. It's cold and raining. We can't. Get back in bed. Get back in bed now."

It was true. It was windy and cold outside, and it had been raining off and on most all night long.

She gave a little and I pushed her back and lifted her legs upon the bed and covered her up... and then I went to the other side and crawled under the covers and lay there breathing hard for a moment. Bunton lay quietly and stared at the ceiling and I felt her body trembling. Her expression was totally noncommittal for a while, and then it was as if a mask had been pulled over her face... a mask that exuded hurt and disappointment. I put my arm around her and tried to pull her to me, only to have her pull away. She turned her back and lay staring at the wall and I felt my heart turn within my chest and begged her forgiveness the only way I knew how.

"Dear God!" I whispered. "All she wanted was to look out at the world. All she wanted was to look down the hill and see the outline of Charlotte's house... to orient herself in the universe. To know where she was, and regain a sense of security." I took hold of her, pulled her to me, and said.

"Come on! Come on... we'll go to the porch." But she pulled away and lay quietly facing the wall, and I lay with my arm over her still body and quietly cried.

CHAPTER FORTY FOUR

Later that morning, Claudette and Jenette arrived and started about doing all the things that needed to be done in the house. They got their mother up, carried her to the den and positioned her in the lift chair where she sat and watched a choice program on the TV. They made the bed, washed the dishes, and put some clothes in the washing machine... and I went to the guest-room and crawled into bed for a little nap.

Then, at some time in the afternoon, one of the girls called the Hospice service and asked that a hospital bed be brought to the house. It was obvious that this was needed. The large poster bed in the master bedroom was not only high and hard for me to get her up and under the coves; it needed some kind of safety rail to keep her from falling off before I could get around and take hold of her.

Almost unbelievable, before I was up and back in the world, Coleman and Reiner were there. They removed the big poster and carried it upstairs just as the worker from the Hospice service arrived with the hospital bed. The hospital bed was assembled and installed, and the girls went about making it up for use. Then, late in the afternoon, it became necessary for them to leave, and I was left to care for Momma throughout the night.

"She's sitting comfortable in the lift-chair in the den," I was informed. "Let her stay there as long as she enjoys watching TV, and give her food if you can get her to eat. Maybe she will drink some instant breakfast before going to bed."

When they were gone, I sat for a moment and tried to talk to Bunton, but she was not interested... she seemed to be engrossed in the TV program she was watching.

I remembered the little under-bed light I had always kept pinned to the bottom of the box-springs in our room, and went in to see if the girls had placed it under the hospital bed. The light was laying on the nightstand. I picked it up, plugged it in and turned the little roller switch. The thing didn't work... one of the girls had turned the switch the wrong way, and apparently broke it.

I remembered that I had a remote control that would turn lights and other plug-ins on, and went to the kitchen to search for it in the cabinet drawer where I usually keep such things. I found the device, went to the spare drawer in the dining room hutch for a battery and returned to the bedroom to put the light together and mount it under the bed.

And then... I heard a loud bang and knew instantly that Bunton had gotten up from the big lift-chair and fallen.

"Dear God!" I screamed. "Dear Jesus"... This was the very thing I had feared the most. I raced into the living room and saw her lying face down on the hardwood floor at the foot of the stairs.

"Oh God! Oh God!" I raced to her, knelt and lifted her and gently removed her arm from its crumpled position under her body.

"Dear Jesus, Dear Jesus" I continued to scream. She was bleeding from the mouth and from a large gash just over her left eyebrow. "Dear God," I screamed again. This ugly cut was up high and near the place where the plug had been removed from her skull when Dr. Fisher clamped off the aneurism.

"Dear God! Dear God!" I continued to cry, as I held her and dialed 911, forgetting the medical alert pendent hanging around my neck... and when the 911 operator answered, I continued to repeat the chant.

"Hello, hello." I heard the telephone saying. "Can I help you? ... Are you alright?"

"Send an ambulance quick," I shouted. "Send an ambulance quick. She fell down... my wife fell down... hurry, she's bleeding badly. Please hurry."

"Is this Mr. Ponder?" She asked. I knew that she was looking at the biographical information the 911 system has associated with the telephone number of each caller.

"Yes!" I screamed. "Please hurry, she's hurt bad."

"How old is she? Is she breathing?"

I was virtually livid. "I can't talk anymore. I've got to call my daughter. Please send someone quick. Please hurry."

I cut the call and pushed the auto button to call Claudette. She had been gone from our house probably less than ten minutes... but it is only about three minutes from our house to hers, depending on the one traffic light at the entrance to Farrah Drive. And, as I later learned, she had already arrived, laid her phone down and went in to take a shower. She did not answer.

I tried Jenette with the same results. Jenette had already crossed Taylor's Ridge and apparently was in the area on the other side where for some reason her phone service is always null.

"Dear God!" I screamed again, as I ran for a towel, a blanket, and pillow and tried to make her comfortable while I wiped at the trickle of blood that still ran down her face.

I tried Claudette's phone again, and she answered.

"Come back... come quick," I said, trying to calm my voice. "Mother has fallen... she's bleeding. She hit her head on the floor. Hurry back... and, call Jenette, I tried but she didn't answer."

Bunton was totally noncommittal. Her face, other than the part that was covered with blood, was white as a sheet. However, she was breathing quite well. I got a washcloth and tried to wash some of the blood from her face. And then, the door popped open and Claudette and Jerry were there.

"We called 911," she said. "They're on the way."

"I called them too… come see if we can sit her up."

We tried to sit her up using the pillow propped against her back, but it was obvious that she was more comfortable lying down. Then, just as we got her in a comfortable looking position on the floor, a first responder from the fire department arrived, followed shortly by the ambulance with the paramedics… and within a short time that seemed like an eternity, we were in the ambulance and on our way to the Redmond Regional emergency room in Rome.

CHAPTER FORTY FIVE

At the emergency room she was rushed into an examination room where nurses, and finally a doctor probed at the lacerations on her face and asked a thousand questions. Then, after a half-ream of papers were filled out with the same information we had given that hospital many times over the last few years, she was pushed into another room and we were told that another doctor would be in shortly.

Of course, it didn't happen shortly... but a doctor finally came in for a moment and advised us that she would go for a scan, and then he would be back to talk to us.

When the scan was completed, the doctor came back in, smiling this time as he approached. He took Bunton's hand and said...

"Well young lady. Looks like all you're going to get out of this is a big old shiny black eye."

He explained that there were no broken bones or other problems related to the fall that would cause any kind of problems.

"However," he said, "there is a little shadow here," he pointed to the right side of her skull opposite the side where the aneurism was located... "that might ought to be looked at later."

"What do you think it is?" Jenette asked.

"I don't want to speculate." He said. "It could be cancer, or a dozen other things." He turned his back and started to look at the wound over Bunton's eyebrow... put on rubber gloves, picked up a small jar that contained some kind of dressing, then set the jar back on a shelf and left the room.

Finally, after another eternity of waiting, a nurse came in and started preparing Bunton for discharge. She gave Claudette some prescriptions and said that we should carry her to her regular doctor, Dr. Joseph Herron within a few days.

When we had Bunton in one of the cars and started back up Highway 27, I did not argue when Bragan who was driving turned on 141 and headed for Jenette and Coleman's house. I knew full well that I should not be at home alone with her. All the other family members who had gathered at the hospital... the whole entourage, were soon at the house talking a mile a minute and making sure that Grandmother was taken care of and comfortable in bed. Then, after a little discussion about who would sleep with her and care for her through the night, I was allowed to go in and lay down beside her.

She had spoken very little since the fall, and I had been wondering, as the others probably had, if that fall had damaged... maybe dislodged some of the work Dr. Fisher had done when he operated on the aneurism. After all, she carried a total of seven little metal clamps in her head.

Jenette came into the room to check on us several times that night and surprisingly enough Bunton only had to go to the bathroom twice. The rest of the time I lay awake worrying... thinking about all the suffering she had had to endure and deriding myself for all the hurt I had caused. And the thing that bothered me most was what I had done to her over the last twenty-four hours.

"Dear God!" I thought. "All she wanted was to look out at the world. All she wanted was to look down the hill and see the outline of Charlotte's house... to orient herself in the universe. To know where she was, and regain a sense of security."

And why on earth did I let her fall? Why did I not know that sooner or later she would figure out how to use the lift-chair control and try to get up and walk?

I took hold of her, pulled her to me, and whispered. "I am so sorry darling... so sorry for every time I hurt you."

She turned slightly towards me and placed her head on my shoulder, and finally I was able to doze off sometime in the wee hours of morning.

The next day, the girls got her up and carried her to the living room where they bathed her face and brushed her hair, and placed a small bandage over the cut in her forehead. And then Jenette brought her favorite breakfast, a glass of instant breakfast with vanilla ice-cream. However, she would not have it. When the glass was put to her lips, she would turn away and say, "Don't want! Don't want!"

The Hospice nurse came, and she too tried to get Bunton to drink some of the chocolate feast, but she would not.

"It's alright." The nurse said. "Her body has been shutting down for some time now. The thing we need to do is to see that she is comfortable, and show her all the love and devotion she deserves. It's easy to see that you and the rest of this family truly love her... and it's obvious that she loves you as well."

She excused herself and went about checking blood-pressure, oxygen level and all the other things nurses do, and I went to the kitchen for coffee and a sweet-roll.

That afternoon the Hospice worker brought another hospital bed and some other equipment to our new location. The bed he had brought to our house in Summerville had not yet been used. After the bed had been installed, the nurse with the help of Jenette and the sweetie-pies made it up, carried Bunton in and did everything they could to make her comfortable.

Up until this time, she had said hardly a word as she sat in the lounge-chair in the living room and watched the TV set. And it was obvious that she had not enjoyed the TV. She had simply sat there and looked at the set and rubbed her hands on the arms of the chair.

"Dear God!" I thought. I suddenly realized that the Hospice nurse knew that she was dying. "Dear Jesus!" I had not fully realized that this was really the reason she had been put under Hospice care. I guess I had just thought of the services they performed as a measure of relief... a service to help with the chores of caring for her through another debilitating illness.

"Dear God, she really is dying. Why? why her? Why not me? Why not me God? I'm the one with all the baggage. I'm the one who has doubted your very existence... who has broken all your commandments. I'm the one who has hurt her God. She has never hurt a living soul... not even people who have mistreated her. You've got your priorities all wrong God. You're taking the wrong one."

I started out the door. I had to get out of there at once. I was surely going to cry, and I wanted to be alone for that. "I'm going home for a while," I said as I passed Jenette in the kitchen... holding back the tears, and trying to keep my voice in check as I passed.

CHAPTER FORTY SIX

That night after sitting by her side and crying the kind of tears one cries deep within his soul, I allowed the girls to persuade me to go to the other guest room and sleep. However, sleep was not the kind of thing I could do at a time like this. I got up throughout the night and eased into the hallway and peeped into her room, only to be discovered by whichever of the girls was sitting by her bed at the time. Usually they would whisper to me and tell me that Mother, or Grandmother, was doing fine and order me to get back in bed.

In the morning, I went to her room and sat for a long time holding her hand, and the world crashed in upon me with an avalanche of memories, dreams, and accusations.

Throughout that day she lay and stared up at the ceiling and I was loath to disturb her thoughts... it seemed that she was busy planning an event that had no room for the likes of me. I held her hand and sometimes she would show scant recognition of my presence. I knew that she was aware that I was with her, and she must have known that I was dying a slow natural death in the knowledge that she was leaving me.

Claudette came in and I asked her to call Jeremy and Terry and tell them not to come just yet. Mother could linger for days, and if they came now, they might have to return to their homes and jobs, only to be required to come back again. She was a skip and a jump ahead of me in that matter. She said that she had already told them to wait.

Throughout that day... that final Saturday before she died, the house was abuzz with people, mostly family members whom I scarcely recognized, Claudette, Jenette, Bragan, Kilie, Reiner, Coleman, and Jerry. Hospice workers came and went, and several friends dropped by. Our pastor, the Reverend David Craven from South Summerville Baptist church, and Jimmy Bryant as well, I think.

Today, that day is a jumble of memories that flash through my mind like a whirlwind. There is no way to dismiss the image of her lying on that bed staring out into space, and no way to untangle all the other sights and sounds that rumble through my mind.

When night finally came, I allowed myself to be ushered into the other bedroom and climbed into bed... and that's when the world turned into a huge panoramic motion-picture screen for the viewing of a kaleidoscope of memories and dreams.

We sat in Daddy's old Ford on Taylor's Ridge and watched a shy new-moon march across the sky... and I managed the nerve to kiss her for the first time.

We sat on the brow... a great precipice atop Lookout Mountain, and watched sun-rays reflect from the tops of lazy clouds as they marched across the green of Shinbone Valley.

I remembered the climb to the chilly top of Clingmans Dome, and the icy fog we combed from our hair as we drove down the mountain to Gatlinburg.

We slid down the hill in cardboard boxes at South Edmonson Street and gleefully climbed back to the top for another ride in our paper mache snowmobiles.

We sat on the balcony of the Casa Loma at Panama City and watched the two most beautiful little girls in the world build sandcastles.

I watched her... this precious one who clings to my memory throughout the long nights as she strolled through surf and sand at Longboat Key, Anna Maria, Daytona, St. Augustine, Mexico Beach, Jekyll, and a dozen other seaside resorts.

I am sitting now looking at a picture of her walking along the beach at Panama City, a picture which I used to create a birthday card for her some years ago. And, although I have never been accused of being a poet, I pinned a little rhyme... a lyric of sorts which, if you will refrain from mordacity, I will write below.

My memory often wanders back

No reason, rhyme or plan

Coming Up The Driveway

I sit and watch you softly walk

In sun, and surf, and sand

It always makes me marvel

God must have had a plan

To let me sit and watch you walk

In sun, and surf, and sand

I love the twinkle in your eyes

When awkward sea birds land

They too seem awed to watch you walk

In sun, and surf, and sand

If I could live another life

Become a brand new man

I'd want to spend it all with you

In sun, and surf, and sand

It's needless to say that finding that little birthday card recently, brought back an avalanche of memories, brought me in fact, to relive her passing, as if it were yesterday.

The day before that awful nightmare was etched into my soul forever... that Sunday before she passed away in the early morning hours, was almost a rerun of the day before. I sat by her bed and held her hand, and rubbed her brow, and kissed her lightly on the lips. At times she would look at me and say words with her eyes that I would dearly love to hear today.

During the day, members of the family were in and out doing all the things families are required to do to keep life in motion. The girls would rotate to and from her room, and the nurse came back and forth throughout the day. She would come and administer medications and make sure that Bunton was as comfortable as possible. When she noticed me wipe a tear, as I did often, she would place her arm around my shoulder and reassure me once again that the fall, for which I blamed myself, was not responsible for Bunton's condition.

Sometime in the afternoon I ventured outside to see if Ooda, my little dog and constant companion, was eating the shrubbery, and I walked with him several times up and down the driveway. He seemed to know that something was not quite right... wondered, I guess why we were not at our house where he could watch for a raccoon, or bark at our neighbors as they passed.

Back inside I sat again by her bed and held her hand and listened without hearing the chatter that ensued in the living room between the girls and the nurse. She came into the room... the nurse, and checked to see if Bunton was comfortable, gave her a small wafer... some kind of medication to hold in her mouth, and a sip of water which she surprisingly took.

I was pleased that she had swallowed the water. I had tried unsuccessfully on several occasions to give her water… but she had always pushed me away saying, "No, no… don't want."

The rest of the afternoon and well into the night she lay quietly and stared into space.

Claudette came in and said that she had to go home for a while, and that we should call her if there was any change whatsoever. She could be back if needed within about twenty minutes. She kissed me on the cheek as she always does, and left.

Bragan and Kilie came back into the room, made themselves comfortable on the extra bed, and ordered me to go to the other bedroom and get some rest. Then, Jenette came in with a milkshake which she insisted I drink and repeated the orders the sweetie-pies had given.

I sat down on Bunton's bed and kissed her gently on the cheek, rubbing my fingers over the ugly bruise above her eyebrow. She opened her eyes and smiled faintly, and her lips tried to say words that only her eyes could utter. I kissed her again and left the room.

However, sleep was not something my troubled mind was ready to allow. I simply lay there and relived a thousand memories and cried perhaps, a million tears.

Finally, when I looked at my watch and discovered that it was almost one o'clock in the morning, I got out of bed and went back in her room and sat on the other bed where the girls were sitting.

The sound of her breathing was different than when I left. She was making a slight wheezing sound each time she breathed in and a near whistling sound as the breath was released.

"I think she is OK." Jenette said. "But, she seems to be having a hard time breathing. I opened the window a little, but it doesn't seem to help. Do you think I should get a fan?"

"We could try it," I answered, and she brought a fan and placed it on the nightstand. But there seemed to be no change in the sound of her breath.

Claudette came back and after a little discussion they decided to call the nurse. I am sure that that nurse was very tired and sleepy at that time in the morning. She had been in and out all day and halfway through the night. However, she was ready to get back in her car and return.

Then, before the nurse arrived, the sound of Bunton's breathing changed again. She started to make a small gurgling sound, and the tension in the room grew as we sat holding her hands and wondering what to do. I had already noticed that the head of her bed was raised to a rather high position, and her head was further elevated with two large fluffy pillows. I mentioned this, and Jenette said that this was the way the nurse had her positioned when she left. She said that the nurse had recommended that her head be kept elevated in that manner.

We sat there for what seemed an eternity, and the gurgling sound increased until I could stand it no longer. Finally, I lowered the head of the bed, removed one of the pillows, and the gurgling sound stopped. She lay quietly and almost smiled as her chest moved gently up and down in a steady rhythm.

"Thank God!" I whispered, as I heard the front door open and the voice of the nurse speaking to one of the girls as she entered.

However, the relief we felt was short lived. Just as the nurse came to her bedside and started to check her pulse, oxygen, and other vital signs, she made a slight gasp for air and then lay breathing small, shallow breaths that grew fainter and fainter within minutes.

My heart jumped out of my chest and sailed out into the universe, as I stood hovered over her and held her hand, and listened to the sound of her going.

She breathed quietly for a time… and, although I cannot be completely sure, I see in memory a faint smile come to her lips, and a halo of sorts drifts through my mind.

And then, God reached down and lifted her gently and carried her home.

FINALLY

As I sit here by her graveside, there is a longing within my heart that cannot be stilled. It is June 10, 2013 and she has been lying here a total of eight long, lonesome months. She has sat on my sheets a total of two hundred forty-four nights... seems a million. My time with her has been an eternity of longing and of togetherness that seemed impossible before.

She has whispered words that bring understanding and a sense of appreciation for the gifts God has provided. She has taught me that doubting God is a human anomaly, peculiar to the Darwinist doctrine and the stupidity of those who follow that creed... a stage of denial that I have never reached in my quest for understanding.

Through the long nights, we have relived so much of the life we had together, and memories linger now through days which are no longer so hard to bear, because she is with me.

We have climbed the heights of Stone Mountain, and swum the cold waters of Allatoona. We have revisited many places we loved and enjoyed in our life together. We have watched our two little dolls ride bareback on Pogo, the little Palomino pony I bought from Mr. Jackson when they were almost too young to ride.

We have strolled through the historic district at St. Augustine and searched for treasure. We have collected Conch-shells on the beaches of Conch Island, and dined by candlelight at a quaint little seaside restaurant at New Smyrna.

She has convinced me that the fall for which I blamed myself had nothing to do with her passing... and that God did not allow her to suffer so many times for naught.

She has pointed me to scripture such as the following.

(Isaiah 38:17) *Surely it was for my benefit that I suffered such anguish.*

(Psalm 119:71) *It was good for me to be afflicted so that I might learn your decrees.*

(Romans 5:3-4) *We also rejoice in our sufferings, because we know that suffering brings perseverance; character; and hope.*

Therefore let those who suffer according to God's will entrust their souls to a faithful Creator.

Sitting here with her and knowing these things brings me to understand that she is not lying here beneath this cold mound of dirt. It is the image of her... the memories of her that continues to bring me back each day, sometimes as many as three or four times, and I will return forever.

I know now that she is there with Mamaw, and Momma, and Daddy, and that precious little Melissa Margret... the third little angle God gave to us in 1952, and then took away before either of us could have the joy of holding her in our arms.

I know that all the questions she used to ask about the place where she now resides are answered.

"What do you think, Henderson? What do you think it will be like in Heaven? Do you think we will know each other? Do you think we will see Mamaw, and Nanna, and the baby? Do you think we can hold her, and rock her, and sing 'Three white ducks'? Do you think she will know us?"

And my answer to her is, yes. Yes darling, I believe that you are there with Mamaw, and Nanna, and Daddy, and little Melissa. I believe with all my heart that you are there, holding that precious little bundle of joy the way you used to hold Claudette and Jenette... and I believe you know that I will be joining you very soon.

I know now for a fact, as I have always known in my heart, that there really is a God; and that, although His word as set forth in the Bible is confusing to mortal man, he is nonetheless the God of the universe and the creator of all. And darling... I know that you are there in His presence.

Ecclesiastes 12:7 - *Then shall the dust return to the earth as it was: and the spirit shall return unto God who gave it.*

She has taught me to look at the fact that I am only human, that I am just like every other human being, and that it was not meant that I should understand God's plan. She has pointed out that Jesus Christ is our real means of contact with God... that He alone gave us the right to salvation... that he gave his life for my sins, and that he has already forgiven all my transgressions.

She has whispered to me in the night... and held me in her embrace, as if she were there in my presence; and I long for the day I will see her again. I long to hold her in my arms and to place my arms around that precious little baby. And, I know in my heart that I will be there soon.

So look down at me darling... look out the window and watch for me as you have so many times before. Hold that little angel up and let her see me... tell her that I will be there soon and hold her in my arms the way you are holding her now.

Watch for me Bunton... watch for me, I am on my way darling, I am coming home, I am almost there. Look out the window darling. Look out the window. Look Bunton... I'm coming up the driveway.

The end

Please turn page

Letters of Praise For

Mary Frances (Bunton) Ponder

By The Ones She Loved Most

"Mama was Unique."

By daughter: Claudette Ponder Mahan

Our mother was a unique person. She was by nature a nurturer. She always saw to the physical needs of everyone in her presence, anxious to make sure everyone had what they needed. I can hear her now, "Want more cake? Are you cold? Come sit in this chair where it's more comfortable".

Mother loved her family. In fact, she loved us so much that she was blinded by it. She always took our side even when we were wrong. She took any hurt that was done to us as a personal affront. She thought we should have everything we wanted. And she wanted us around at all times. She spent many hours driving me to piano lessons, waiting in the car, listening to me practice, and attending recitals, for which I will always be grateful. And, boy, did she love Daddy! She always made sure that he had something good to eat. (Mother was an excellent cook and cooked all the time). She made sure that everything he wore was ironed, so that he would look good at all times. Even when he was just going into the yard to mow, she insisted on ironing his jeans.

Mama was faithful to take care of all her loved ones. She loved and cared for her mother and all the people who had raised her. She spent many years taking care of their needs when they became too ill to take care of themselves.

She loved little children, and always said that if she became suddenly wealthy, not that she would buy diamonds or furs or houses, but that she would build an orphanage.

~~~~~

"Oh, I can't wait!"

By daughter: Jenette Ponder Slay

"Oh, I can't wait to tell Mother that!" Every time something good or exciting happened, I would immediately think that. Mom was always pleased and happy when something good came our way. Our happiness was her happiness. And though she has been gone eight months, I still find myself thinking, "I can't wait to tell Mom."

Mother touched each of our lives: husband, daughters, sons-in-laws, grandchildren. She was the hub of our household. She was the planner, the coordinator, the administrator of activities. She nursed us, coaxed us, drove us, and praised us. She made every holiday an event, every celebration special.

Mother had an attitude that said, 'If you're going to do something, do it right', and an abundance of energy when she was working to accomplish any task that improved our lives. She was meticulous and precise and would give us only her best!

She always amazed me with her photographic memory. She knew the words to a million songs and some of my fondest memories are of her singing as she worked around the house. Sometimes she would get stuck on a jingle and would drive us all crazy and would laugh and sing it again when she realized we were going bonkers! She could tell you what everybody at church wore on Sunday down to the number of buttons on a particular dress or the color of the preacher's socks.

She was the Betty Crocker of our family. Her meals were delicious and when we were children, she demanded that we eat homemade biscuits and eggs before we went to school. Her cakes were excellent and she made sure that we each had our favorite on our birthday. As I write this, Mother's birthday is only two days away and I wish I could make her favorite cake for her.

Was Mom successful? Did she accomplish what she wanted to in life? I know that some people measure success by fame or worldly treasures. Some measure by wealth. I consider that Mom was a most successful woman. But not measured by false fame, treasures, and wealth. I think her success was in her family: united, secure, cared for, and loved. I believe she would agree.

~~~~~

"Grandmother Was Always Busy."

By Grandson: Jeremy Mahan

Grandmother was always working. As a little boy I remember going to Granddad's office and seeing her working as his receptionist. At home, she kept the cleanest house in the world....you could, as they say, eat off the floors. She was always busy cleaning. But the best work she did was her cooking. She was the best cook ever, bar none. Her specialties were fried chicken and chocolate cake. She loved to cook for all of us, especially the grandchildren.

One memory of Grandmother was how she always fussed at Granddad about his inventions. I remember the time she opened the oven and found the evidence of yet another of Granddad's experiments.....two BIG rocks. What he was trying to prove, I don't know, but Grandmother wasted no time in getting them removed.

When she wasn't working, Grandmother usually could be found in the porch swing singing to a grandchild. Grandmother loved her grandchildren.

~~~~~~

AUTHOR'S NOTE

It's needless to say that I should have told Jeremy that I was trying to enhance the color distribution in a couple of pieces of Rose Quarts.

"She would sing me to sleep in the porch swing."

By Grandson: Terry Mahan

Grandmother and Granddaddy's house sits back in the woods up a long driveway over a deep ravine. It was just like a nursery rhyme from a children's book. As a child, I would sit with Grandmother outside on their large covered patio. She would sing me to sleep as we rocked in the porch swing. I can still hear her singing "Six White Ducks" and calling me "Pumpkin". She loved us grandkids.

Grandmother cooked three meals every day. She was the best cook to ever grace a kitchen. She was especially skilled at making fried chicken. Going to eat at grandmothers was like having Thanksgiving Dinner every meal.

I will always miss her.

~~~~~

"I know I will see her again someday."

By Grandson: Reiner Slay

I'm not sure if I can sum up, in just a few sentences, how much Grandmother meant to all of us. From her sense of

Humor to her love of spoiling her grandchildren, Grandmother always made it clear that her family was what she cared about most in this world.

It is still hard to accept that she is gone. She was always a constant in my life. No matter what was going on in the world or in my life Grandmother was always there to make me smile and offer me food. I can still see her shaking her fist at me and pretending she is going to beat me up if I don't behave. She never could shake her fist for more than about five seconds without cracking a smile.

It is often said that you don't know what you have until it's gone. That may be true in some cases but I'm certain that everyone who had the pleasure of having Grandmother in their life knew just exactly how special she was. We knew it because she made sure we all knew how special we were to her.

I know I will see her again someday. She is walking and talking with Jesus right now and when I get to heaven she will give me a big hug, offer me food, and tell me how glad she is to see me. I love you Grandmother. Always have and always will.

~~~~~

"Grandmother was my best friend."

By Granddaughter: Bragan Slay White

What better tribute can I offer to my grandmother than to tell you that she was my best friend? Even though her

Health was bad, she had an attitude of fun. She loved to act silly with us and was constantly saying funny things.

After I came home from my honeymoon, she said, "I don't like that."

"Why?" I asked.

"Because you didn't ask me to go with you!" And I think she was serious.

My grandmother had a lot to do with who I have become as an adult. Her work ethic, her attitude about doing your best, and her devotion to family have all influenced my life. I will always be grateful for her loving, caring attitude. I miss her and will never forget her.

~~~~~

"She was a very special lady."

By Granddaughter: Kilie Slay

"Six white ducks!" How many times did grandmother sing that song to us? I remember that song and the squeaky sound of the rocking chair. Reiner, Bragan, and I would take turns rocking with her and sometimes Granny, as we eventually began calling her, would rock us two at a time. She never seemed too tired to give us another turn.

She was silly and funny and loved to act goofy with us. She always made Bragan and me a chocolate cake for our birthday and would drive all the way to Birmingham, Alabama to bring it to us. Reiner's favorite cake was Italian Cream and even though it took a long time to make, he got one every birthday. The night before her brain surgery was her birthday and we have pictures of all of us eating birthday cake with blue icing and making funny faces.

She loved taking us shopping and could never say no to us. She loved going out to eat together. She loved iced tea and desserts of every kind. She liked swinging on the porch and going for rides. She loved the color of the fall leaves and the sound of the ocean. And she loved to sing.

I began calling her Granny instead of Grandmother because she pretended that she didn't like that name. I continued to call her Granny because she was fun and loving and very special to me. She was a very special lady.

~~~~~

Comment.

By Great Grandson: Luke Mahan, 11 years old

When I went to visit Great-Gradmom, she always told me to sit in the orange chair. I don't know why—I suppose it was because it was directly across from her.

There was a candy dish on the table next to her chair. She always gave me some.

~~~~~

Comment.

By Great Granddaughter: Kate Mahan, 8 years old

When I saw Great-Grandmommy, she always gave me candy and lots of hugs.

~~~~~

Comment.

By Great Granddaughter: Taylor Mahan, 5 years old

Great-Grandmommy had CANDY!

~~~~~

Memorial.

By Great Granddaughter: Aria Slay, 23 months old

~~~~~~

Bunton in 1947

<<<>>>

Mary Jim put her hand out in a gesture of recognition and said, "Henderson Ponder... Mary Frances Gilmer."

"Oh no!" I whispered to myself. "Not another Mary Frances." But, my mind was chanting. "Mary Frances, Mary Frances. Dear God, this is the one."

"Her nickname is Bunton" Lou Cindy said.

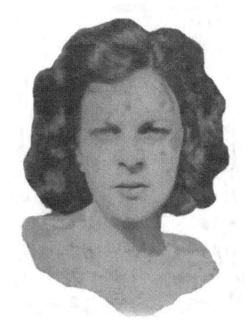

"Bunton! Jesus... I whispered." But I was really thinking, "What kind of mother would call a beautiful creature like this Bunton?"

One cannot look at the girl in this picture and not believe that she was created by a loving God... and that she is resting in His presence at this very moment.

Henderson Frank Ponder grew up in a three-room cabin along the banks of Raccoon Creek, near the little cotton mill town of Berryton Georgia.

Recently, he went back to visit the old home place for the first time since moving away in 1941.

As he walked out to the remains of the storm-seller, he remembered the smell of straw beds, jam on fresh bread, and the rumble of storms that never seemed to harm.

"There isn't much left of the old home place after all these years. Just an old chimney, a few concrete blocks, a pile of rocks and a hole in the ground.

Look again! Look at me... Not much left here either."

Ponder served two terms in the U. S. army during the WW2 era.

He's a member of the National Society of Public Accountants with more than 60 years of practice.

He lives alone in a small cottage in the north Georgia mountains.

MESHA

Mesha was only fifteen years old when Germans SS officer Heinrich Peeler and his men came to Yugoslavia and requisitioned the ground floor of the Covanich home for an office. However, she matured fast when she witnessed her mother and one of the Germans in sexual embrace on the living room couch.

She ran away to join her uncle Peter, who was making a name for himself as leader of the Covanich Group, a remnant of the Mihailovich underground known as "The Chetniks."

Little did she know that she too would find love when Frank Henderson, a young American officer was assigned by the OSS to assist the underground in the acquisition of weapons and supplies.

However, love was only one emotional extreme she would encounter as she and Frank traveled the snow-covered mountains of Montenegro and witnessed the pain, suffering, and despair war can bring.

SAN MARIO ISLAND

FRANK HENDERSON was surprised to learn that his old war buddy Mario Sisconi, eldest son of a New York City mafia family, had named him principal heir of his estate when he died.

Mario had lived quietly during his retiring years on a small private island in the Caribbean Sea. Frank was even more surprised when he arrived at St. Thomas Island to pick up Mario's sailboat, only to learn that other members of Mario's mob had their own ideas about who was entitled to Mario's bounty.

Followed out to Mario's island by the mobsters, Frank soon found himself in captivity, subjected to the cruelest forms of torture as Mario's former cohorts tried to force him to reveal secrets he did not know.

During the ordeal, memories of the war and the experiences he and Mario shared left him with little peace of mind, even when the torture ended

JUDISCHE JADE

FRANK HENDERSON struggles with the onset of dementia as memories of the war, and especially memories of the girl he loved and the German officer who caused her death course through his mine.

As he works to repair the big sailboat his old war buddy, Mario Sisconi left him, Frank believes he sees the German officer in question entering the harbor at Charlotte Amalie.

This story will carry you through the mountains of Yugoslavia where the author served with the Mihailovich underground during the war. It will introduce you to Myeshka (Mesha) Yolanda Covanich, a young freedom fighter who deserves your honor and respect. You will become acquainted with Heinrich Peeler, former assistant director of the German Schutzstaffel who amused himself by carving little artifacts from the dried bones of Jewish babies.

You will feel the pain and suffering the author feels as he tries to bring forth in vivid detail long fallow memories of love, hate, fear, and despair.

And you might cry a little, too.

THIS BOOK IS AVAILABLE AT BOOK STORES AND ONLINE BOOK VENDERS AROUND THE WORLD ISBN 978-1-4357-2959-9
BEST BUY AT http://www.lulu.com/shop - SEARCH BY TITLE

Made in the USA
Columbia, SC
11 October 2021